THE ROAD TO ELSEWHERE

Anthology of Award-winning Short Stories

ISBN-13: 978-0-9742652-7-8
ISBN-10: 0-9742652-7-6

DEDICATION

This anthology is dedicated to those who visit Elsewhere daily

To the authors featured in this book: Scribes Valley thanks you for your time, patience, trust, and talent.

TABLE OF CONTENTS

ELSEWHERE BOUND
A Foreword by David L. Repsher, editor

Greetings! This is your captain speaking. We hope you are enjoying your journey to Elsewhere. We are currently cruising at an incalculable altitude, traveling at an immeasurable speed, and we are on schedule.

Oops, did I say 'schedule'? Wow, my mistake. In Elsewhere, there are no schedules. No timetables. No agendas. No calendars. No clocks. Time does not matter. We have no ETA, and no arrival date. But, that's okay. Elsewhere is always open.

Now, for your information, there are a few things you should remember after we arrive in Elsewhere. First, you are on your own. What you do and what you see are up to you. Every one of you will have a unique and different experience, so there is no need for the "herd mentality" there.

Second, there are no borders in Elsewhere. No fences, no boundaries, no "Keep Out" signs. You are free to roam wherever your imagination takes you.

And finally, rules are non-existent in Elsewhere. You will be limited only by what your mind allows. So, I urge you to sit back, relax, and open your mind. Allow nothing to hinder you as you explore that fantastic, unbounded, unbridled, wide-open place called Elsewhere.

Thank you for attention. This is your captain, signing off....

FIRST PLACE

EMPTY SHOES

"Empty Shoes" is for my sister, Donna, who inspires the world.
--Tricia Spencer

For ninety-two years I've loved gray days. There's always been something about thick, heavy clouds and slightly damp air that comforts me. I enjoy the way the grayness hugs my shoulders like a tenderly crocheted afghan and the way the air smells forever clean. I'm backwards, I suppose, since most people wish for bright, warm, sunshiny days. Folks seem to liken sunless days to depressing bad moods and "get it over with" times. But gray days have never been that way for me. That is, until today.

Today, I am as gray as the sky, and it's not just my advanced years, mind you, nor the thin white fluff of what used to be a thick mane of honey blonde hair. It's not even the translucent parchment paper skin that now wraps my insides in a way-too-delicate cocoon. No, it's deeper than all that. My life of spirited involvement and adventure now feels like the waxy blob of a burned-up candle—golden memories snuffed to nothingness by the bleak, irreversible grayness that has settled over my heart.

And this trip to the park isn't helping like I wished it would. It has always helped before.

I've always loved this wilderness park, so full of its woodsy scent and tangled trees. Just feeling the bark at my back as I lean against an oak twice my age feeds my soul like nothing else has ever done or ever could do. I've been luckier than most. I've always understood my connection to the earth. Those not blessed with that understanding drift willy-nilly through life, living then dying without a speck of internal peace, without any real knowing to comfort them. I've seen it happen so very many times. You can't get to be my age without watching a lot of folks fall and blow away into just a memory. Ashes to ashes and all that. So I am indeed lucky. My roots shoot out the bottoms of my feet just like the oak, grabbing the earth, embracing its lifeblood, holding me steady and firm in the face of any storm.

But this storm may be too big, even for me. Even oaks can be torn from the earth sometimes.

My hands look funny to me now. They're gnarled and twisted, but they still work. Sure, I've had to change the way I hold a cup or wield a knife, but I still get the job done. That's more than some can say. Here in the park, as I look down, my hands remind me of the bark of my favorite tree. Lord, they're crusty. I think I should have used an industrial strength moisturizer all these years. Oh, for heaven's sake, I'm making myself laugh. 'Industrial strength moisturizer'—who ever heard of such a thing?

I wonder if anyone hears the rustle of the colorful leaves scurrying from my path as I trudge through them. October leaves are such a rich treat. Reds and oranges, browns and yellows, clinging to their branches with all their might, trying to show the world that against all odds they can survive the bitter winds of the winter to come. But in the end, year after year, their efforts are in vain and they tumble and turn to nothingness. It's not a terrible thing. It's just the cycle of life. Brightly colored leaves die and depart in a brilliant sendoff, drifting softly to the earth where they thin and crisp and crumble before scattering away to parts unknown.

I feel a bit crisp and crumbly myself. I can only hope that my own exit will be as beautiful as the departure of the leaves and that folks will find themselves "ooohing and ahhhing" over my own recycling. Dancing through life then singing your own swan song is the cat's meow of living and dying, if you ask me. Of course, I'm not dead yet. Slow. But not dead.

I haven't cranked up my knees to run in too many years to remember, but I still traverse the ground without a cane. That has to say something to the world about my own triumph against the odds. I'm caneless. Bravo! I suppose that wouldn't seem like such an accomplishment to the ladder-climbing masses who judge victory by the size of their house or car or bank account. But to me, caneless is an enormous triumph. I wonder if 'caneless' is even a word. Doesn't matter. At ninety-two, you get to speak any word that pops out of what is left of your brain and no one will correct you. It's one of the perks of antiquity.

This trail is my favorite one in these glorious woods. Here, oodles of small animals still dash to and fro, free and busy, unaware that progress is closing in on them faster than it has any right to. I love the animals. I love them more than anything. Animals are pure of heart and soul. They don't know meanness for meanness' sake. They don't know shame and haven't got a clue about vanity. They can talk to your spirit without ever uttering a sound. What's not to love?

Oh, there's Brisket! I knew I would find him here. I swear that squirrel's got his ear to the ground and knows the minute I step one bony foot down this path.

"Hi Brisket! How's the fall gathering going? Hope you're socking away a barrel full 'cause my rheumatism says it's gonna be an icy one this year."

That Brisket. He's such a sweet fellow and so industrious. Too bad most men couldn't claim those traits. Oh, but there was *one* man. Now dang, I feel that grayness squeezing my heart again. And I'm not gonna cry. I can't cry, 'cause if I did the tears would chap the furrows of my cheeks until they were as stiff as a rusty washboard. Then I'd be in for it. There's nothing more miserable than a ninety-two-year-old chapped cheek. Smooth-skinned cheeks don't know how good they've got it. Velvety soft skin can take a good tearing up with no problem, but wrinkled cheeks just wither under those dang ruthless tears, drying and trapping the salty brine in ruts too deep to scrub out. Next thing you know, it feels like someone's planted a row of watermelons on your face. So crying isn't going to happen, regardless of how gray my heart may feel.

Harry was a good man. No, a *great* man. He loved animals too. And he loved me. I loved him right back for nigh on to sixty years before he, too, went ashes to ashes and left me alone in the world. I got by though, 'cause I had a home full of animals to love and tend, and I never felt as alone as I guess I really was.

Harry and I still talk regular. Death doesn't really part you, you know. It's just different. If I ask Harry a question, I can't actually hear his answer now, but I feel it just the same. Of course, that may just be because lately I'm durn near deaf as a post. Harry could be screaming at the top of his lungs from the great beyond, and my hard-as-a-walnut eardrums wouldn't catch more than a whisper. Old age can be a challenge. But I'm caneless, so I won't complain.

I think it's almost sunset, but since it's so gray, I can't be sure. Sunset, whether you can see the pinks and blues streaking by the horizon or not, is a fine time of day, a peaceful time. Harry passed on at sunset, and it was right fitting for a man of his fine, gentle worth. Who could ask for a better way to go? He just kicked off his shoes, leaned back in his patched-up leather easy chair and went to sleep. I never saw his dusky blue eyes again. And that's a loss of gigantic proportions, for Harry's eyes were a sight to behold.

Oh, I wish I'd brought a hanky. Stupid tears are trying their

TRICIA SPENCER

best to plop from my tired eyes. Miserable things. A body should be able to say when and if tears get to fall down your face. My sleeve will have to do, but then it's worked just fine many times in the past, so I figure it can take another soaking, if need be.

I think I'll pull up a rock for a rest. This trek gets harder all the time, especially now as I tug Harry's old army sack along. And besides, watching Brisket work is like rubbing sweet oil into my aching muscles. That critter just makes me smile, and I think now is a very good time for a deep soul smile.

I miss my animals, who one-by-one up and left me to go live with Harry until it was just me and Buster left kicking about. Buster was a bossy pigeon with the proud demeanor of a peacock. Sweet, silly bird. By all that's understandable, he should have gone a long time ago too. His wings didn't work right anymore so he couldn't fly worth a darn, and his feathers looked half plucked most of the time. But he hung on—for me, I think—until his little nineteen-year-old heart finally creaked to a halt and his toes reached for the heavens.

"You'll love it out here, Buster. I promise. Brisket there will watch over you 'cause he's just that kind of guy."

I don't know if Buster can feel me patting the duffle bag, but I think he can. Even dead things can feel, I believe. Maybe not like us living things, but somehow.

That little rest felt good, but I better be off before there's no light left at all. Just a little further and I'll be at the perfect spot, there by the river where the water gurgles around slick, silvery stones.

I'm confident I won't trip and fall as I make my way in the waning light, for even though my shuffle hasn't got any get-up-and-go left in it, the osteoporosis has conveniently trained my eyes on my feet. Now I can watch every step without casting my gaze up and down like an overworked elevator. It's good to know there's a silver lining in everything, even osteoporosis. If it weren't for silver linings, life would be unbearable sometimes, maybe *most* times.

"Here we are, Buster."

Pulling Buster from Harry's bag, I hold his stiff little body close to my chest one last time before I kiss the top of his black head, wrap him in the brand spanking new towel that I spent all this morning embroidering his name on, and lay him at my feet. I'm going to have to get on my knees to bury him. I can't dig with my gardening trowel unless I'm close to the ground. Oh, I know it will be hard to get up again, but I'll deal with that when the time comes. I've always dealt with life's relentless obstacles one step at a time.

As I dig, I can faintly hear birds calling and cooing, and I wish I could hear their songs loud and strong. Dadgum ears. Hearing is a fine sense, one that can fill you up with joy from the tips of your toes to the top of your head. It's a sorrow to lose it. But I remember well the sound of music and laughter, animal purrs and yips, the hustles and scurries of the park's creatures below the whispering wind, and the deep, rich timber of Harry's voice. I just play those memories in my head when I want to hear something precious, and it's almost as good as the real thing. Truly. Besides, I'm caneless. No call to complain about not being able to hear so very well when a body's caneless.

There. I'm done, and Buster is at rest, on this green earth at least. Somewhere else, he's no doubt soaring, ebony wings spread wide, his feet tucked into his belly for a smoother flight. The image makes me smile, and yet another tear threatens to erupt and spoil the moment. I can't seem to hold the weeping back now that they're all gone. Harry, my friends, my animals, all gone. It's just me now. Me and a fate worse than death hanging over my head.

A nursing home.

People I don't know decided I can't be me anymore. I'm too old, too frail, and too stupid, I guess, to take care of myself. I've done it for more than seven decades in my own home—with

Harry and without—and now courts and nameless faces have ordered that come Monday I'll be moving. Good thing Buster decided today was a good day to die 'cause "caring" caretakers decreed that animals can't live in the Home, no matter how long they've been family. I think Buster knew what that meant and he just couldn't bear the thought of such a painful goodbye, so he went to Harry.

"Oh, Harry, don't these people know I'm caneless? Caneless, Harry!"

I look down and find I'm holding Harry's shoes. I didn't even realize I'd pulled them from the bag. I knew I was going to get them out. I just didn't know my hands would do it without me thinking about it straight on. I reckon something just kicks in at times and we do things without mulling them over first.

Harry's shoes are big and empty, just like the day he kicked them off to lean back in that worn old chair for a nap. They're real fine shoes in real good shape. Harry took care of his things, and what he didn't take care of proper, I did. That was our way. We took care of each other, 'cause we lived deep in a mighty kind of love.

Blasted tears. They're getting Harry's fine shoes all wet, At least, they must be. I can't really see them too well now that it's getting on the back side of sunset, the light that skipped and twinkled across the river's flow now swallowed by ever-widening shadows. And as the weary day reaches for its restful night, I find the grayness didn't soothe me as it always has in the past, not in the face of so much loss. I think that maybe that's why some folks don't like gray days. Maybe they know that one day the grayness will just wash right through you, taking your colors with it, and there won't be any turning back from that point on.

I'm not turning back. No, sir. Dancing through life and singing your own swan song, that's what's right for me. *I* choose what's right for me. *I* say where I will live, how I will live, and who will live with me, animal or not. *I* say. I am me as long as I draw breath. I am caneless even if most others don't recognize what that means.

Harry's shoes look proud sitting atop a little bird's grave. I know somewhere Harry is smiling. I can feel his smile just as I can hear his heart speak to me.

The earth feels cold beneath my toes as I slip my own shoes from them and set them before me. Brisket scampers over to investigate this new offering, and he's almost close enough to touch, but I know that won't happen. Yet, he doesn't move on either. He just sits up, his cheeks stuffed to the gills, and stares at me. I smile at him, and though I can't see him well in the heavy shadows, I think he's giving me a big squirrelly smile right back. Bless his free heart.

My small shoes look extra teeny next to Harry's big ones, but they sit just as proudly at attention, their toes pointed to where in just a dozen hours the sunrise of a new day will begin. Yes, four empty, tear-stained shoes will make fine vanguards.

Getting up from my knees is harder than I remembered it would be, but the tree next to me graciously lends its support. Very fine things, trees. Everyone knows they can be counted on to cleanse the earth's thick air or offer shade from a merciless sun. But it's their stature that really matters, their vigilant silent reminder to us all to stand tall and strong. I am reminded now.

My hands cling to mossy clumps that clamor up the tree's side like ready-made handles, and finally I'm upright once more. Well, as upright as my body will go these days.

It's been a swift sunset, and the trees and bushes are shrouded with inky heaviness. Gray days always seem shorter than sunlit days, for they quickly meld into black nights. I can see next to nothing, but my shoeless feet feel the wetness of the riverbank and that's all I need to know to reach my destination. Seeing and hearing would just be a bother now anyway.

My eyes are dry. All the tears, and all the years, are spent. They were good years, and it just wouldn't be right to top them off in an animal-less "home" where nary another living soul would be caneless like me. My housemates would be stretched out on colorless sheets with a never-ending view of a badly spackled ceiling. I've seen them, the light gone from their eyes, their feet aching for a touch upon the real earth. They may still be breathing, but they aren't living. And they will die on someone else's terms. No, that would never do. Not for me.

One last glance back to see the shadowy form with the bushy tail resting atop two regal pair of empty shoes, and I know I've made the right decision. Brisket knows it, too, for he has an intriguing new home to store treasures in. Even empty shoes have a silver lining.

As for me, I say when. I say how. I say where. I've earned that right, and no one will take it from me.

Here.

Now.

I turn toward the water and walk straight and proud and caneless into it, singing my own swan song to the trees and birds and critters of the park. And I sing to Harry, my precious Harry, who I know is running barefoot toward me even as the water laps higher and higher up my legs, twisting my long skirt into soggy billows that add pounds to my meager weight. That's okay. Extra pounds are nothing to worry about. Extra pounds will be just fine.

I've had many adventures throughout my ninety-two years, and I've learned something valuable in every moment in time. Life has been a respectable teacher. I even learned that there is joy and peace in an old pair of empty shoes, a most surprising and comforting lesson. I've learned so many skills and facts and figures and procedures that my sponge-like brain is fair to bursting with knowledge. But I didn't learn it all.

As the fates would have it, I never learned how to swim.

And today, that's just another of life's unexpected and blessed silver linings.

About the author:

"Empty Shoes" is the second Tricia Spencer short story honored as a finalist in Scribes Valley Fiction Competitions. Finalist, "Noses, Toes and Elbows" was recognized in 2005 and appears in the Scribes Valley anthology, They Do Exist!

Tricia received the Best Nonfiction Book award for *Tips, The Server's Guide To Bringing Home The Bacon: The Customer Speaks To Every Waiter, Waitress and Restaurant Manager in America!* from the Southwest Writers International Manuscript Competition where the final winners were chosen by a Penguin Group editor. *Tips* is available on Amazon.com and elsewhere and has become a training manual for restaurants and food servers around the country. The 2002 book received a second printing in 2006. Her short story, "Deviled Eggs," was a winner in both the L. Ron Hubbard Writers Of The Future Competition for Science Fiction and CrossQuarter Publishing's Paul B. Duquette Memorial Short Science Fiction Contest. "Deviled Eggs" is published in *CROSSTIME*, the 2002 science fiction anthology featuring the winners of the CrossQuarter competition. Her short story, "Miracle Man," was a winner in the 2005 Cloak and Dagger Mystery Writing Contest where the finalists were judged by renowned mystery author Jeremiah Healy, aka Terry Devane. In 2007, her nonfiction short, "Spirit Prayers For Joyful Living, A Gentle Path To Spiritual Well-Being" was published as an AMAZON SHORT on Amazon.com.

Tricia's life pursuits reflect her philosophy that variety is truly the spice of life. From food service to touring with the International Company of *Up With People* to creating and marketing her own line of wedding accessories to author, with a world of diverse and creative pursuits in between, Tricia has reveled in the highs and lows of self-evolution and in the myriad of endeavors life has to offer. She is listed in "Who's Who of American Women", "Who's Who of Emerging Leaders", "Who's Who in The West", and "Who's Who in The World."

Born and raised in Central Illinois, she and her husband,

Mark, now live in Southern California where they share their home with all manner of furry and feathered creatures. They also share a passion for the simple pleasures of life, like sharing a great meal or taking a drive through unknown territory. Visit her website at: triciaspencer.net

SECOND PLACE

TWO, ONE
©2009 by Kandice Powell

Your eyelids become illuminated with the sun's "hello," and you carefully open them to decipher the brightness of the day. Your eyes are vacuums to the sight of the water-damaged popcorn ceiling, then to the red-plaid flannel sheets, to sucking in the vision of the strange boy sleeping next to you. Humiliatingly roll your head back and mouth an "oh my God." Slink out of bed without disturbing the flannel, and slip back into your New Year's dress. In one swoop, gather your coat, purse, and shoes, and turn to the door. The strange boy's loud snore obliterates the quietness like a gunshot in the deep woods. Like a deer, freeze and look up to the headlight eyes of another boy bunking above your bedmate. He gives you a smile, you half-smile back, and gallop out of the dorm room in your bare feet.

Week One: It's a boy. The gender, blue eyes, and mahogany hair color are already determined.

In Calculus class, raise your hand to answer the problem the professor has written on the board. It is the beginning of a new quarter, a new year, and you need to redeem how you rang it in. Confidently walk up from your front row seat to the chalkboard and illustrate the steps of resolution. As you write the numbers and mathematical signs, unnecessarily pronounce the steps aloud, in hopes of impressing your professor. Your political science graduate of Harvard dad taught you the art of persuasion and you devoured all professional speaking and educational advice he gave you. Declared correct, you return to your seat, and cross your legs in your designer jeans.

The professor dismisses the class, and you trek your way to Starbucks to meet your boyfriend. He apologized to you last night for the fight on New Year's Eve. He wants you back, and feeling light and loved once again, you eagerly boomerang yourself to him. Walk in your Christmas gift snow boots through the remnants of the morning's wholesome snow, and notice that near the street it is turning black. Soon it will be your third-year anniversary with your beau, and he is oblivious that you aren't white snow anymore.

Week Three: The brain and backbone are created and the boy is growing faster every day.

You get your first exam in Calculus back. You aced it. Satisfied with yourself, you slip it into your folder and exit the classroom. In the crowded hallway, play bumper cars with the other students till you reach the penetrating January wind outside. Retrieve your cell phone from your book bag and listen to a voicemail from your dad at home. He just won Iowa. You are proud, and realize your family has earned another few inches height on their pedestal. Choose to receive this status. Call your dad back to congratulate him and announce your good news: delegated director of your sorority's annual service project—The March of Dimes.

Week Five: The boy's ears and eyes are forming and signs of his mouth are developing. The boy has his first heartbeat.

The bowl of your toilet, instead of your usual coffee mug, welcomes your morning face. Pull out the register tape in your mind to go over the list of food items you ate last night. Sushi never made you sick before. Diagnosing yourself as having the flue, groan as you get up from the bathroom floor. Mope down the hallway as if your head weighs more than your body. Reach for the cup of Sprite on the nightstand beside your bed, take a sip, and place the cup back on your opened planner. Look through the clear drink to the bottom of the glass. The circular cup is placed on your red-circled day, two weeks ago. You still haven't started.

Week Seven: The fingers and toes sprout from the boy's hands and feet. The boy has his first bowel movement.

With your oversized sunglasses and sweatshirt hood concealing your head, you enter the clinic. The doctor affirms what you knew was true, and you sit in silence in the examining room by yourself. Then you realize you aren't by yourself. Cry an "oh my God."

Week Nine: The boy is understanding movement by dancing and can grasp with his fingers.

The last visit to the clinic was your dress rehearsal. Once again with your hood cradling your face, you walk around the corner towards the clinic. Let the snowflakes fall on your eyelashes and linger for a few seconds. Think how each chaste snowflake will dance like a young ballerina as it descends to the sidewalk. Then it will be tainted black by the dirty street. Every other step is a battle; you're clawing at your own heart. For that second you want to turn around. You think of telling your boyfriend, your dad, your community. It's too hard. Take another step. Rationalize that you'll just hurt yourself and you won't hurt them. What a burden for them to fight through. Wonder if you are the only one being sacrificed. The odd step it is to the door, is the step in which the battle leans toward keeping your appointment. Shake the snow from your boots as you enter the clinic. You sit. You wait. You sweat. The doctor calls your name. You pray.

Week None: The heartbeat has stopped. No dancing. No fingers grasping. No more growth. No more icy blue eyes, mahogany hair.

Leave the clinic with less. Feel empty at your core, like a pumpkin prepared for carving. You're waiting for a sense of relief, satisfaction of knowing that you protected everyone. The wind has picked up now and the icy snow splinters your swollen eyes, so you bow your head down at the sidewalk. Your feet meet the black snow and you take a step onto the street. The black snow doesn't protect you from the orange flashing hand on the other side of the street. A car horn snaps your sunken head up, and instead of staring into the sharp slivers of ice, you wait being shattered by an SUV screeching its tires to stop short of hitting you. The salt crunches, the brakes shriek, and before you can feel the heat of the tires rubbing the road, you are sharply grasped by a hand around your left arm bicep, branding you like a barbed wire tattoo.

You are safe.

Catch your fleeing breath, and search around yourself frantically for your Saver. See His back towards you, as He walks away down the street. Watch as He vanishes in the crowd of people waiting on the corner to see the white figure leading them to move.

About the Author:

Kandice Powell is a soon-to-be graduate of the University of Cincinnati, and a soon-to-be mother. This is her first published short story, and though her major and experience is in the Marketing field, she plans on continuing to write. Kandice is a soccer guru, and thoroughly loves every aspect of the game from playing to coaching. She also enjoys being active and outdoors, and trying new sports like surfing and snowboarding. In addition, she has high aspirations to travel around the world, and share her heart to serve in South Africa, and experience her passion for ancient history in Greece. Kandice is happily married to her husband Shannon, who is responsible for pushing her out of her safe-zone, and challenging her to see that the only limits on her capabilities are the ones she sets for herself. Kandice and her family live in Cincinnati, Ohio; home of the less than par professional sports teams. Kandice is truly thankful for the gifts she has been given, and being able to share them with others. Hopefully, you'll read more from her soon.

THIRD PLACE

MA BATES
©2009 by Ronna L. Edelstein

Norman Bates' mother is rotting away in the storage room under the basement steps. Vera knows that, just like she knows that Tall Paul, the cutest boy in the ninth grade, will never ever ask her out. Fourteen-year-old Vera has known about Old Lady Bates for the past year, ever since Dad had naively taken her and her older brother to see *Psycho*. Vera knows that if she dares to enter that storage room, her skin will peel away and she will become a grimacing skeleton—just like Mrs. Bates.

Vera knows a lot of things. She knows her older brother does not miss her, even though he is now a college freshman and living on the nearby campus. He never talked to her when his bedroom was across the hall from hers so why would he start now? Vera knows that high school will be just as bad as junior high, only now she will not have to ride the school bus and listen to Sandy, Carol, DeeDee, and all the neighborhood girls sing their special "We are the Stanton girls who wear our hair in curls" song, and be the only one from the Stanton neighborhood excluded from both the song and the club. And Vera knows that Ma will find some reason for her to go down those bare steps into the darkness of the basement with its tomb-like storage room.

"Vera! Vera!" Ma shouts. "Run down to the storage room and

bring me a can of peas and a can of corn for dinner!"

Dad understands Vera's fear. After seeing Norman Bates' frenzied stabbing of his naïve motel guest, Dad is relieved Vera can still shower without fearing a knife slicing through the plastic shower curtain. Ma, however, lives in her own microcosm where the only things to fear are being fat, having no money, and receiving a grade of A- or lower.

"Vera! Get the cans now!"

"Please, please, let me be okay!" Vera repeats this mantra as she drags herself to the basement steps. Her legs play tug-of-war with her; they want to stay upstairs, but she needs them to safely deliver her to and from the storage room. Vera turns on the light switch, but the forty-watt bulb only awakens eerie ghouls from their cement-walled prison. She has begged Ma to buy a bigger bulb, but frugal Ma has always dismissed Vera's request with a "what a waste of money" remark. Ma's constant references to "money doesn't grow on trees" and "we're not made of money" once caused Vera to ask Dad whether they were poor. "No, honey," he had explained, "Ma just remembers growing up during the Depression when her family didn't have a lot of extra money to spend on luxuries." Luxuries? Vera does not understand how a brighter bulb, one bright enough to blind Mrs. Bates from seeing her, can be seen as a luxury.

"Vera, hurry up! I need to heat up the vegetables!" Ma's voice cuts through the darkness, a lightning streak of impatient words.

It doesn't matter to Vera that Ma is in a hurry. It doesn't matter that the basement steps don't creak, that loose boards don't gnaw at her shoeless feet, and that sharp nails don't pierce her fragile soles. None of this matters because Vera knows what awaits her once she reaches the bottom and makes that left turn into the storage room: Mrs. Bates. Old Lady Bates is much worse than Snow White's stepmother or the Wicked Witch of the West. Vera cringes from mocking mirrors and water that will cause her bones to disintegrate into a dark puddle. Vera knows she needs to outgrow these fears, but she cannot help believing in mirrors that tell her she is not the fairest, in witches that melt, in classmates who sing songs without including her and have parties without inviting her—and in mothers like Mrs. Bates.

Vera bends her neck and peers into the storage room. Everything is where it belongs, just the way Ma likes it. Cans of pears, peaches, pineapple, and fruit cocktail fill the shelves to the right, while cans of applesauce (why can't Ma buy the chunky kind that Vera likes?) crowd the shelves on the left. Directly in front of Vera sit rows of vegetables. She grabs two cans, one of peas and one of corn, holding the green tin in one hand and the yellow in the other to use as weapons in case Mrs. Bates decides to make an appearance. Then, slowly backing out of the room, Vera pivots, races to the steps, rushes up the stairs, and slams the cans on the kitchen counter.

"Vera, there is no need to make so much noise. Did you remember to turn off the basement light?"

Vera stands mutely. She stares at the vegetables, willing them to burst from their tin cages and grow into mammoth green and yellow monsters that eat Ma and drip their juice on her, sending her to the same watery death that destroyed the Wicked Witch.

"I turned the light off," Vera lies. Then, without another word, she leaves the kitchen, vowing to never eat one pea or one kernel of corn for the rest of her life.

Not that she will be able to eat dinner tonight, anyway. Vera almost wishes Mrs. Bates had gotten to her so she will not have to face the dangers of that night. Every freshmen girl except Vera has looked forward to this night from the minute they graduated junior high last June. This is the night when they will find out which high school social group, a preview of the college sorority, has accepted them. They will know once and for all where they stand on the popularity hierarchy.

Each neighborhood, including the one Vera has lived in forever, hosts a get-together at the house of one of the seniors. After an evening of final scrutiny by the older girls, the president/hostess distributes one of two envelopes: a welcoming one with the name of the new social group embossed on it; a blank one with the implied "Don't call us, we'll call you" message.

Vera already knows where she stands on the social ladder; she hasn't even reached the bottom rung and she probably never will. She is almost comfortable with this reality, almost content to spend her evenings and weekends reading *Little Women* or watching television with Dad. If it were not for Ma, Vera would right now be in her pajamas and curled on the couch. But she knows that Ma needs more from her. Ma needs Vera to not only bring home the A's, but to also be popular. From stories her aunt has told her, Ma, despite her academic success, had always been a drooping dandelion in a field of blooming roses when it came to friends. Ma needs Vera to be different—and better.

"Milt, Vera, dinner's ready!"

Even before Vera unfolds her napkin or takes one bite of strained applesauce, Ma's words make her feel queasy as if she has just ridden the Tilt-a-Whirl at Kennywood.

"Milt, Vera has her big evening ahead of her!" Ma proclaims as she joins Dad and Vera at the table. Ma had begun the countdown for this "big evening" a week ago, starting every meal with a reminder to Dad. "Tonight, she'll find out which of the high school sororities has asked her to join."

"Ma, they're not sororities," Vera tells her for the ten-zillionth time. "They're just these stupid clubs that the girls join so they can wear the same sweater to school or exchange notes in some kind of secret code." Of course, Vera does not add, "And it's not which one I'll be asked to join, Ma. You and I both know that I won't be asked to join any."

"And, Milt," Ma continues as if Vera has not said a word, "once Vera's in, maybe we could invite the girls to a party. If the weather's nice, you could grill hamburgers and hot dogs, and I could bake my Toll House chocolate chip cookies. Won't that be nice?"

Dad nods, but Vera senses that he knows, just as she knows, that Ma is again living in her fantasy world where Vera is a five-foot two-inch blonde with blue eyes and a dimpled smile, not a five-foot eight-inch Amazon with dull dishwater eyes and a smile that reveals an overbite that no braces will ever correct.

Vera can type seventy words per minute, thanks to Ma who had sent her when she was only ten to a summer business school, but Vera cannot conquer any of the latest dance steps. Even at fourteen, Vera understands the irony of having dancer's legs but being unable to walk across the room without tripping over her size ten shoes, let alone do the twist, jitterbug, or whatever other dance is the current rage.

"Ma, I can't eat any more. May I be excused so I can get dressed?"

"But you didn't even touch your peas or corn!" scolds Ma. "Oh, well, go get ready. I'll let Dad do the dishes so I can come and help you."

Of course, you will, Vera thinks. A closed door means nothing to her mother. "You have nothing I haven't already seen," she always chuckles as Vera tries to cover herself with her bedspread.

Still, Vera closes the bedroom door, takes off her blouse and pedal pushers, and slowly faces the mirror attached to her dresser. Ma likes mirrors. She likes standing naked before the full-length mirror in her bedroom and turning around like a ballerina atop a music box. Holding in her nonexistent stomach, Ma scrutinizes her anorexic body for any signs of fat from the meat, potatoes, and vegetable dinner she only nibbles. Vera tries to escape mirrors, but she finds that as impossible as avoiding the storage room under the basement steps. How can she tell her popular locker mate, the one assigned to share the space with her, that the magnetic mirror she has hung inside the locker always sneers at Vera with an all-knowing "you are a loser" look? How can she tell Grandma that she loves the compact she gave her but that she pasted contact paper over its mirrored lid so she will never have to see herself?

Vera stands before her looking glass enemy and examines herself. She only just got her period, years behind every other girl in her class, so her breasts still look like two small pebbles pasted onto her sunken chest. Vera longs for breasts that will fill a sweater and cause Tall Paul to look her way. She has tried stuffing her training bra with two of Grandma's hankies, but the right side always comes out more lopsided than the left. A black mole, resembling a dried-up raisin, sits above her left pimple-like breast. Although it provides color to her otherwise ghostly skin, that mole seems to embody everything that is wrong with Vera's life.

"I hope you turn cancerous right now and kill me before I have to go to this dumb club or sorority or whatever thing tonight!" Vera tells it but, of course, it just sits there, a black raisin indifferent to her pain.

"Vera, you're not dressed yet!" Ma barges into the room, leaving the door open behind her. Does she care if Dad happens to pass Vera's room on his way to the bathroom? Not Ma, who only last week shouted to the cleaner when he had come for the dirty clothes, "I'll be there in a minute! I'm only in my Maidenform now!"

"Vera, wear your red and white striped blouse with the matching shirt. You always look so nice in that."

Vera knows that this outfit makes her look like a barber's pole, only less round, but she also knows that arguing will be futile. With Ma still hovering, Vera snaps on her padded bra and squeezes into her cotton undies. Her blouse hugs her skin; naturally, the mole peers through the white stripe as if Vera has dripped mud onto her blouse. Within minutes, Vera has transformed from a photograph fading with age and disuse into a red and white pole, a peppermint stick, a Fourth of July firecracker—anything but a fourteen-year-old about to be asked to join one of the high school's popular groups.

"Vera, you look so nice. Have a nice time—and let your hair down!"

Dashing out of her room, Vera air kisses Ma good-bye. Dad, like Sir Lancelot, awaits her at the bottom of the steps. He holds her coat for her and, pulling her close in a hug, whispers, "No matter what happens tonight, I will always love you."

Vera never doubts that. It is disappointing Ma that has her shaking. Ma expects her to be like Susie, the girl down the street. Only a year older than Vera, Susie has a boyfriend (the Tall Paul of her grade), is on the cheerleading squad, and is already the secretary of one of the most popular clubs. Susie does not get all A's, but she also does not have a mother who runs around half naked when the cleaner rings the bell. "How can I be like Susie, Ma, when all I see is you and what you aren't?" Vera has asked herself this question for years without ever getting an answer.

Returning her dad's hug, Vera walks out into the night, the starless sky matching her dark mood. Just as she reaches the bottom of the steps, she once again hears Ma call through the screen door, "Just try to let your hair down!"

"Let your hair down!" Vera repeats in her best Ma voice. Vera has heard those words for years, ever since her first school dance and first family reunion. Any occasion with a social aspect to it always comes with Ma's "let your hair down" advice. The first time Vera heard those words she was only about seven or eight; she wore her brunette hair in a pixie style that turned her into a tall Peter Pan. The young Vera did not understand how she could let her hair down when she had so little hair to begin with. Now, a wiser Vera gets it. Ma wants her to have fun, relax, and be everything Ma was not and will never be. It would almost be easier to tug the short strands of a pixie cut until they became long tresses than try to be part of the "in" crowd. Yet, if getting into the social group will make Ma A+ happy, Vera will try to put aside her fears and let her hair down.

Vera walks past Bobby's house. Although two years older, he and Vera used to spend summers on her porch and build magic lands with Ma's *Mah Jong* tiles and racks. Every year Bobby would go with Vera and her family to Kennywood for the school picnic. He never even minded when Vera got the first ride on the roller coaster with Dad because he knew Dad would ride again with him. Vera treasured Bobby not as a boyfriend but just as someone who liked her. Then, when Vera was leaving sixth grade for junior high, her brother—the same brother who had chopped off her favorite doll's hair while assuring her it would grow back—told Vera that Bobby only played with her 'cause he liked Ma's Toll House cookies, lemon Jell-O pie with graham cracker crust, and roasted Kennywood potatoes. Vera did not want to believe her brother, but how could she argue with someone who always made the highest honor roll and had graduated both junior high and high school as class valedictorian? Thanks to her brother, Vera spent the past two years trying to avoid Bobby. Not being in the same school made that easy, but now Vera will be starting high school. She worries Bobby will see her in the hall and look the other way and that she'll cry and everyone will call her a baby.

Crossing the street, Vera passes the Lewis' house. Mr. Lewis, a former gym teacher, once spent hours teaching Vera how to do a forward roll. How proud Vera had been when she could finally do what all the other sixth grade girls had mastered months and even years before! Of course, the day she showed off her forward roll, the others had already moved on to backward rolls, cartwheels, and headstands. Vera knows that those tumbling, somersaulting athletes will be the gold medalists in tonight's social club Olympics. She knows she will stumble home once again steps behind her peers.

Even before Vera turns the corner, she hears the loud, guttural voices of Mr. and Mrs. Steinman. They are the only couple in the immediate neighborhood without children; they are also the only couple who speak English with thick, sometimes indecipherable accents. Dad once told Vera that both Mr. and Mrs. Steinman came from Germany and had been sent to a camp after Hitler took power. At first, the young Vera imagined her summer camp, a glen of green grass, towering trees, blue lake, and unlimited bug juice and s'mores. As she matured and began to read books like *The Diary of Anne Frank*, she redefined camp. Vera now imagines the Steinmans' camp as a huge basement filled with row after row of Mrs. Bates clones.

Even though sympathetic towards the Steinmans, Vera still

fears them. Their voices bark like the two German Shepherd dogs owned by Dr. Levine. Mr. and Mrs. Steinman may simply be asking each other about his or her day or may be commenting on a book she has read or a radio program he has heard, but Vera always interprets their words as ones of anger. Whenever Vera complains to Ma that she cannot do an errand because she worries about being caught in the cross-fire of the Steinmans' verbal battle, Ma always laughs at her and tells her that words never hurt.

Ha! Sticks and stones may break bones, but words hurt—a lot more. "Here comes Vera the beaver!" Freddie, the chubbiest boy in her class, always announces when Vera walks into the room. Vera clenches her lips, trying to hide her beaver-like teeth from the jeers of her classmates. "Hey, Vera, how's the weather up there?" Hours later she thinks of the perfect response: "Cleaner than the air you're polluting down there!" But at the time, she can only lower her head, like a turtle trying to disappear in its shell. "Wow, Vera, did oars come with those shoes?"

It always takes just one cruel taunt to destroy Vera. She no longer loves her new loafers with the copper pennies shining in them. She no longer cares that Jackie Kennedy, the glamorous first lady, also wears size ten shoes. She wishes her tormentors would eat every mean word in the English language and then explode from a vocabulary overdose. She wishes Mrs. Bates would leave her storage room cell just once so she could stuff Freddie and his friends with sharp-edged words and then gleefully clap her skeletal hands as they choked, gagged, and bled.

What really gets to Vera is that Ma is also a word villain. Vera knows she means well, but when Ma tells Vera she will never win a beauty contest, when Ma insists that Vera can never be too thin, and when Ma asks if Vera really and truly likes her hair that way, Vera feels as formless as Dorothy's scarecrow without his straw. Even if she were deaf, Vera knows she would still be able to hear Ma's words by reading her eyes and smelling her anger.

Vera knows she is nearing the house where Judy Drake, perpetual Queen of Homecoming, coolest president of the coolest club, and hostess for the evening, lives. She knows because the personality of the street has changed. This part of the community boasts larger homes than her neighborhood; the lawns have received professional care, and every bush has been cut to the exact same height. Vera's mom and dad own a car, but these parents have two cars, all more luxurious than the pale blue Chevy with its creamy roof belonging to Vera's parents.

Every year Grandma buys Vera a new first-day-of-school outfit; every year Ma, ignoring the after-Thanksgiving and Christmas mobs, takes Vera shopping to get the best bargains. No outfit, however, turns Vera into the fashionable "American Bandstand" dancers she envies or the Susie or Judy Ma wants her to be. Clothes hang on her long frame as if she were a human coat hanger. Vera constantly pulls at her skirts to make sure the elastic waist band (Ma only believes in elastic due to its stretching capabilities) does not snap and leave Vera running through the halls in her cotton Hanes underwear.

Vera knows she is nearing the house because, unlike the dark night, lights illuminate it. Lamps turn the windows into yellow smiley faces, just like the ones her teachers draw on her essays and tests. Vera knows that these friendly smiles are not meant for her. Even the rainbow balloons decorating the trees seem to droop like deflated rubber leaves as she slumps by them. Judy and her cohorts have drawn a "Welcome Freshmen" banner and hung it over the front door. Part of Vera applauds how neatly the artists colored within the lines, but another part wants to rip down the banner and wrap herself in it like a mummy and then crawl into a crypt and be forgotten forever and ever.

"Let your hair down," Vera hears Ma say. "I will always love you," Dad whispers. Vera looks up at the sky, wishes upon a nonexistent star, and makes her way to the front door.

Mrs. Drake, as blonde and perky as her daughter Judy and a woman Vera cannot ever imagine in a Maidenform bra, greets her. "Vicky, how nice to see you!" Mrs. Drake gushes.

Vera does not even bother to correct her.

Mrs. Drake leaves Vera alone, an unwanted stepchild intruding upon the happy family. Vera, determined to let her hair down, takes a step or two into the room and freezes as if numbing drugs are being injected into different parts of her body. Four other Veras, also frozen, stare back at her from the mirrors that cover every wall of the living room. Each Vera shares her sprayed bouffant coiffure, the result of sleeping every night with pink rollers painfully piercing her skull. Each Vera wears her red and white striped outfit with only a muddy brown spot on the left side of the blouse marring its pristine look. Each Vera moves her eyes back and forth, tiny spotlights searching for the real Vera and a safe way out. The tangible Vera knows only one thing for sure: this room of mirrors, not Mrs. Bates' storage room under the steps in the basement, is hell.

Hell assaults Vera's senses: shoes jitterbugging against the hardware floor, gossip spewing from reddened lips, flowery cologne competing with the aroma of hot-out-of-the-oven brownies, perfectly flipped hair bouncing up and down. Vera tries to integrate the cliques of girls. She tries to remember that she has known these girls all her life. But tonight, they are as strange to her as she is to them. Tonight, there will be no letting down of hair.

Vera's mouth feels desert-dry, but she avoids the sunshine yellow cups filled with Coke. She fears she will burp or that the Coke will add another stain to her red and white striped blouse. Needing something to do with her hands, Vera grabs a peanut butter cookie, breaking it into tiny pieces until crumbs fill her napkin.

She thinks of home. She longs for the safety of her bedroom where she can sit at her desk and practice her already perfect typing or crawl into bed and finally begin Pearl Buck's *The Good Earth*. She knows Dad is watching television or pretending to read while really thinking about her. She knows Ma is vacuuming, something she always does when she is tense. Vera hopes that the vacuum's wire turns into a poisonous snake that wraps itself around Ma's throat, or that Ma will become locked forever in a horror house of mirrors. Vera knows Dad will hug her, but what she really wants is for Ma to bury her fantasies and accept the reality that she has a daughter who will never ever let her hair down.

Vera leans against one of the mirrored walls, hoping that she, like Alice, will be able to disappear beyond the looking glass. She hopes the other Veras will hide her in their embrace, but, like her, they seem unable to escape from a room of mirrors. In one mirror, three Carols laugh at a story three Judys are telling. The real Vera hears only bits and pieces about red glasses and a train of toilet paper trailing from a skirt. Vera wants to cover her ears with her hands, fearing Judy's next words will be about the peppermint stick girl glued to the wall, but she cannot move. She cannot move even when Linda and Laura and Lisa come so close to her that she can see the one tiny freckle dotting the pale scalp of Linda's part and the rubber band vibrating on Laura's braces and the beginning of cleavage peeking out of Lisa's blouse.

Vera exhales, providing the air for Linda, Laura, and Lisa to inhale. She senses the connection she has with them; she understands they are the daughter Ma wants—the one whose only flaw is a tiny freckle, whose imperfect teeth will be straightened by braces, and whose cleavage begs for the laciest, most beautiful Maidenform bra ever made. Vera wishes she were Linda, Laura, Lisa, Susie, Judy—anyone but herself.

Vera stands there until the clock strikes nine p.m. and Judy and her friends turn out all the lights. A few of the freshmen giggle in pretend fear, but Vera relaxes for the first time. No light means no mirrors. No mirrors mean no reflection or other Veras.

Judy then turns the lights back on. "New freshmen!" she purrs. "Please proceed to the basement while the rest of us prepare for the final event of the evening—the distribution of the envelopes."

Hell has just become more hellish. Not only does Vera have to peel herself away from her corner sanctuary, but she also has to descend into the basement. She hopes that Mrs. Bates, used to

Vera and her imperfections, will fear the Drakes and their perfection. She hopes that both she and the mirror shatter into so many pieces that Mrs. Drake has to ask Ma and her vacuum cleaner to help sweep up all the imperfect shards. She hopes that the perfect Drakes do not have a storage room under the steps.

The Drakes do not have a storage room. They do, however, have a large basement, bigger than Vera's room, her brother's room, and her parents' room all combined. With its phonograph and stack of records in one corner and its pictures of Frankie Avalon, Sandra Dee, and Annette decorating the walls, it is obviously the setting that gave birth to Judy and molded her into her perfection.

Vera spends the next hour watching all the Judy clones dancing, eating brownies, slurping Cokes, and promising to still be best friends even if they get into different social clubs.

At exactly ten p.m., the hour when Vera usually falls asleep with the light on and a book in her hands, she and the others return to the living room. Judy and her mirror images have turned it into a fairy land lit by candles and scented by flowers. The older girls stand in a circle around a card table covered with a shiny blue cloth. Rows of envelopes, too white to belong in the blood-red of hell, are lined up on the cloth.

After thanking everyone for coming, Judy invites each freshman to take her envelope and to have a great high school experience.

Vera walks home past the Steinman's, where voices, now slightly subdued, can still be heard; past the Lewis's where the youngest daughter is always practicing her handstands, past Bobby's house where Bobby has probably locked himself in his room away from his mother and her weekly *Mah Jong* game.

When she reaches her house, she fumbles in her purse for her keys but makes no effort to unlock the front door. Vera knows what awaits her. Dad will wake up from his pre-bed nap, and Ma will rush to greet her until she sees the sweat-stained white envelope, the one with the blank surface, clutched in Vera's hands. Ma will shake her head, sigh, and know that once again Vera has failed her.

Vera turns from the porch and walks along the cement pathway to the side door. She quietly inserts her key and tiptoes down the steps to the basement. She doesn't care that Norman Bates' mother is rotting away in the storage room under the basement steps. She doesn't care that if she dares to enter that room, her skin will peel away. Vera doesn't worry about Ma searching for her and finally finding her, a skeleton amidst a grocery store of tin cans. Vera finally knows she is safe. In this storage room without mirrors, she does not have to confront the person she is—and the person she will never become. She does not have to see disappointment in her daughter cloud Ma's eyes and cause Ma to shrivel up until she and Mrs. Bates become one.

About the author:

Ronna is a daughter and mother, a teacher and student, a reader and writer. Although she has traveled extensively, she welcomes spending her "golden years" in Pittsburgh, the city of her birth. She begins each day at the gym, exercising only on machines that allow her to read as she works out. Most of her days end at one of the city's many theatres where she volunteers as an usher. As a part-time faculty member of the University of Pittsburgh's English Department, she spends four days/week as a Writing Center consultant. This year, Ronna also has the pleasure of teaching Freshman Programs, a one-credit course that introduces students new to Pitt to the rich opportunities of both the University and the city. Despite her busy schedule, she always finds time to spend with her close friend and roommate—her 92-year-old father.

"I thank Dad for teaching me that a cold chocolate phosphate in the summer and a hot cup of Ovaltine in the winter can ease all problems; Jonathan and Ilana for reminding me that the past does not have to define the present or the future; and Ma for allowing me to make real her teaching and writing dreams."

HONEYSUCKLE DREAMS
©2009 by Chandra Prater

Sarah shaded her eyes against the hot afternoon sun. Michael was bent over the truck with his head under the hood. He had taken his shirt off as the day grew hotter and dust had stuck to his sweaty back. His Levi's were faded and covered with dust.

"You 'bout done, honey?" Sarah called.

Michael raised up, a wrench in his hand. There was a smudge of grease across his cheek. Sweat ran freely down his face and strands of his dark, curly hair were plastered to the side of his face. He turned his brown eyes toward her and she felt her heart leap. After fifteen years he could still do that to her. "Maybe twenty minutes," He called back.

She sat down on the porch swing and gazed out into the hot Tennessee afternoon. It was mid-July and summer was in full bloom. The faint, sweet smell of honeysuckle drifted on the breeze. The truck radio was tuned to a classic rock station and the music played softly. Sarah leaned back and closed her eyes. She thought back to the first time they met.

She had been a junior in high school, he had been a senior. He had sat by her at a pep rally and found it amusing that despite all the cheering and screaming, she had remained absorbed in her novel.

"Whatcha reading?" He grabbed her paperback and turned it over to reveal the cover, a man and woman in a passionate embrace and the title *Forbidden Desire* embossed across the top.

He chuckled and she blushed deeply.

She was struck by his dark good looks and soon found that he was easy to talk to and had a great sense of humor. It wasn't long until they were a couple and Sarah found herself deeply in love.

They lived in a poor rural area where financial struggle was a daily fact of life. College was out of the question and most students graduated and immediately took a job in a local restaurant or a store and worked their way up to a plant or foundry in a nearby city. After she graduated, Sarah got a job working as a waitress at Leon's Family Restaurant where she still works today. Michael got a job at Charlie's garage and put his high school auto mechanics classes to use.

Sarah was twenty years old on that starry April night when he looked into her eyes and asked if she would spend the rest of her life with him. She couldn't imagine it any other way. She knew without a doubt that he was the one for her.

It hadn't always been easy. Charlie Morgan, the owner of the garage where Michael was employed, decided to move to Nashville and try his hand at becoming the next Garth Brooks. Michael tried desperately for months to find another job and it was a very stressful time for them. They argued a lot, but always ended up in each other's arms, dreaming of better days.

Michael finally secured a job in nearby Chattanooga at a foundry. They were able to move out of their mobile home and into a small house with a big yard and had lived here ever since. He had always been there for her through good times and bad. He was her rock, her strength, her life.

Sarah opened her eyes and looked at the driveway, empty except for her beat-up Buick. She had sold the truck a month after Michael's accident. Too many memories. The smell of honeysuckle was still in the air, but the truck, the radio, and Michael were only one of the many memories that played like a video in her mind. She wiped her streaming eyes, stood up and walked across the porch and back into her lonely house.

About the author:

Chandra Prater lives in Tennessee with her husband and two teenage sons. She enjoys reading anything she can get her hands on, writing, and traveling the country with her family. "Honeysuckle Dreams" is the first of her short stories to be published.

NEWTS
©2009 by Devin Murphy

At the bottom of the escalator to baggage claim, a mass of people were waiting and Chad didn't recognize her at first. Her hair had flowed past the middle of her back since they'd been married, since he'd known her. Even when she wore it up, there was a blond fringe on top of her head, and he loved pulling out the barrette and letting it fall over her shoulders. Now it stopped just below her ears and he felt a sadness worse than having been away for so long again. Worse than missing her so much. Like now, even that he was back, he'd come back to the wrong place.

She pushed her way towards him and they hugged at the bottom of the escalator. He picked her up and swung her around the way he always did when he came home. Every four months they'd swoon together in the same spot like silent film stars.

"Your hair, you didn't tell me about that." Both his hands were on the small of her back, holding her to his chest.

"Do you like it? I wanted to surprise you," Mandy said.

"I love it," he said, throwing his handbag around his shoulder and wrapping an arm around her neck as they waited for his bags.

When they got home the sound of the television hung in the air like the constant noise of a bad party. He walked into the den as Mandy paid the babysitter. His ten-year-old son Gill was sitting cross-legged two feet from the television. His hair was brushed straight back and was thick and blond like his mother's. Gill didn't turn from the television.

"Hi, buddy," Chad said. "Daddy's home." He squatted down on his knees next to Gill and placed a hand on Gill's back.

Gill jumped away from him like he'd been burnt.

"Whoa, buddy! It's just dad. It's daddy."

Mandy charged into the den, "What happened, Chad?"

"I just touched him, that's all." He looked at Mandy apologetically and turned back towards Gill. "I'm sorry, buddy. It's daddy. Daddy's home." He pulled a small toy ship from his pocket and handed it to Gill. Gill stayed in a crouched position, leaning away from his father.

"You know it takes awhile, Chad," Mandy said, walking up behind him and putting her hands on his shoulders. "Just leave him the toy and he'll take it when he's ready."

"Here you go, buddy, I got you a ship like the one daddy works on." Chad left the toy cargo ship on the carpet next to his son.

Chad sat down in the chair behind Gill, and Gill sat back up in front of the television. Gill loved car chases and was watching C.O.P.S now. They were running video of a drunk reeling off into the night with red and blue lights flashing through the dark after him. Gill was sitting two feet from the screen again and when the drunk's tail lights wobbled from their straight red course and went skidding off the road and flipped, Gill leaned even closer. When the car rolled, Gill screamed again. It was a scream like a last gasp for air.

"Chad!" Mandy's voice rose from the kitchen. "Don't touch him yet." She walked into the room and saw him sitting on the recliner. "Oh. Car crash, huh? Sorry." She draped herself over the armrest so she was in his lap, and kissed him.

He ran his fingers through her short hair and thought of how it used to sway back and forth across her back when she walked. He'd miss how, when she was on top of him in bed, her hair would hang down like a wall and hide everything but their two faces.

"Do you really like my hair?" Mandy asked.

"I love it, honey. Why don't you put Gill to bed so we can be alone? I'll show you how much I love it." He kissed her again, grabbing the back of her head and cupping it in his hands. Pulling his face away, he saw Gill looking at them. "Hey, you. It's Daddy, it's okay."

Gill was staring just as intently at them now as he had at the television.

They took Gill to his room and Chad watched as Mandy changed him into his pajamas and put him in bed. Chad saw that his pajama pants were almost too small for him now.

"Good night, Buddy," Chad said from the doorway.

Gill just looked across the room with a blank stare until Mandy leaned down to kiss him. Gill turned back towards her, his eyes wide open, reached up both arms for a hug, moved his hands to the back of her head, lifted his own head closer to hers, and slipped his mother the tongue.

"Jesus!" Mandy jumped away from him like he was a snake. As she walked out of the room Chad saw how pale her face had become. Gill's eyes were wide open as Chad walked out and shut the door. Gill started screaming as soon as the door had shut.

"Leave the door open a crack and keep the hall light on," she said from down the hall before she went into her bedroom. Chad opened the door and Gill stopped screaming.

Mandy brushed her hair at the night table as Chad sat on the edge of the bed and felt the soft down comforter sink beneath him. It was cool against his legs. He gripped his knees and watched Mandy in the context of her things. The room smelled sweet and fragrant from her basket of clear perfume bottles. Tubes of creams and moisturizers sat on a shelf. She had an unlit candle on the windowsill in the corner, and she'd thrown a thin, tan and blue paisley scarf over her lampshade.

He'd spent his adult life watching her brush her long hair at night, and when he was at sea he went to bed thinking of her brushing her hair, as he knew her preparation was the true invitation. Her hair now covered all but the tip of her earlobe and it felt strange to see her shortened strokes for the first time, though her neck was tan and he wanted her now just as bad as he always did when he came home.

"Come to bed, Mandy," he said, lifting the covers.

Mandy stayed at her table and kept brushing her hair. "Chad, I'm sorry. God, that was the worst thing yet. Did you see that? That was disgusting."

"He didn't mean it. He was just doing what he saw us do. Now come to bed."

"Jesus, Chad, he stuck his tongue down my throat. I can still feel it. Eeww." She shook her shoulders like a shiver ran down her spine. "That was awful."

Mandy got into bed, but didn't want Chad to touch her. So they talked about where he'd been, and what she'd been doing for the last three months. Then she fell asleep and he couldn't. He still wanted her and couldn't sleep because of the want.

Chad left the bed and looked in through the open door at Gill sleeping. He walked to the kitchen and poured himself a glass of apple juice. The sweet taste coated his mouth. He sat down in the open kitchen with the darkness permeating in from outside. He was tired from the long flight home. By morning, the ship he'd just left, the *Coral Sea*, would have unloaded its freight of four-hundred-some-odd Toyotas and would be pulling out of Charleston Harbor, back into the open Atlantic en route to Hong Kong. The men he'd worked with around the clock for the last three months would go about the work of the ocean; each wanting and needing everything they idealized about home in the absence of their homes to match the hunger that comes from being so alone for so long.

The next morning, Mandy woke up early and found Chad at the kitchen table. She rubbed his shoulders until he woke, then she started making breakfast to welcome him home, and for Gill's tenth birthday. When they were all dressed later in the morning, they walked down the street and through the Oakwood Cemetery where the back side of the property slopes into Cazenovia Creek.

Mandy took Gill's shirt and shoes off and covered him in sunscreen. Gill walked into the water with a small plastic cup. He walked slowly, like a heron, moving each leg inches at a time, reaching into the water with one hand to flip over a rock the way Chad had shown him. He'd gotten good at lifting the rocks so they wouldn't stir up the silt so he could see the little red newts. He'd place the cup behind them and use his hand to scare them backwards into it.

Gill screamed each time he caught one. He held up the cup and looked at his parents where they sat on the bank. The inarticulate bellowing echoed across the water, and he carried the small cup to the shore where he emptied the water and the little lizard into a bright red plastic beach bucket used for making sand castles.

"Good job, Gill," Chad called to him as he watched the little red streak of the lizard flow from the boy's cup into the bucket.

"That's a good one, Gill," Mandy said, and then she grabbed Chad's hand. "I'm sorry about last night. That just made my skin crawl, you know. Caught me off guard."

"That's okay. How's he been doing, anyway?"

"Nothing's changed—nothing changes. You know how he is. Give him another day or two and he'll warm up to you again. It always takes time, you know that."

"I know," Chad said.

Gill stopped moving and stood knee-deep in the water, looking up at the birds flying overhead. He stood pole-straight and honed in on that one patch of sky, even after the birds cleared the trees and were out of sight.

Chad knew Gill would stand there frozen until he unhinged by himself. Today, though, part of him wanted to grab the boy and shake him, scream at him to say something—anything, scream at him that his father was home.

It had been a hard night. Chad woke up angry and he wanted to take it out on someone. Watching Gill, he figured if the boy was a mute that would be fine—though he wasn't. Chad imagined all the navigational charts he'd ever seen clumped together to make a hulking mother landmass, Pangaea, before the break and shift of continents. He imagined the first versions of man waiting in a quarter-darkness for dawn. Chad thought that the noises Gill makes must be similar to what those first desperate and confused men must have sounded like.

Gill would always speak in grunts and cries and it was in the inflection you had to find meaning, never in words or the start of words. If he was a mute that would be fine, it would be settled, but it was some hidden block that always had the potential to lift, which was so crushing, as the hope was a false hope that would not die, just linger like a dead horse in sweltering heat.

"I hate when he does that," Chad said while watching Gill in the water.

"You hardly ever have to deal with it." Mandy said, with a trace of anger in her voice.

"Look, I don't want to start a fight. You know I miss you guys and want to be here when I'm not."

"I know, but you do this every time. You're gone for three months and then expect everything to be great as soon as you come back. It takes him time to get used to you, and I hate seeing how much it eats at you when he acts like you're a stranger."

"Well, shit, Mandy, I just want to come home and be with my family—have my son welcome me home. Is that too much to ask?"

"Chad, I'm stuck here taking care of him every day and I hardly get much more, with the exception of him trying to make out with me last night. That's how it is."

Gill screamed in the water. He'd unfrozen from staring after the bird and caught another lizard. He carried it over to the bucket and emptied the cup into it.

"What do you expect to find? What is it you want so much, that never lets this be good enough for you?" Mandy asked him. "It's hard to love you when you are away, Chad. You know, I get a few phone calls from god-knows-where from you, and I never tell you the half of what it's like here by myself. Then you come home for a while and want everything perfect. Well, we can't deliver like that."

Chad thought of those phone calls he'd made to her. How he ran to the nearest phone booth in every port looking to make contact with some voice that would be happy to hear from him. He'd lift the receiver, letting it ring and ring, letting that moment of wanting mesh into the thousand nights he'd spent adrift that would be lost if he had no one to tell of them to.

He was remembering all the sea-beacons he'd rounded that blurred into the dark backdrop of water as he passed. He wondered how he could tell his son of having tested his body and soul, tell him that he knows they both break and mend many times. Sitting with his wife, he felt like he was coming upon the knowledge that the harmonious tune of oceans hinted at, that this was his time of trial, and trial, and trial...

Walking back to their house, Mandy and Gill walked ahead of Chad, who carried the bucket of lizards. He watched them as they swam over each other or tried floating on the surface as the water sloshed back and forth. He put the bucket on the blacktop next to the house's side door and went inside. Mandy was cleaning Gill, and Chad could feel all the old hurt and fights they'd had brimming just below the surface of their talking to each other.

When Gill was clean, Mandy went to the store. Chad sat with Gill, who was watching the movie *Smokey and the Bandit*. Gill would come to orgiastic states of joy when the cop cars would plow into each other, and white-sided cruiser after cruiser would pile up in the last scene. And though the music played all the way through the movie, it was the steel grinding into steel Gill was tuned into.

Mandy returned as the sun was setting. She had a birthday cake and called them into the kitchen for it. "What did you do with those lizards, Chad?" She asked, as she stuck ten colorful wax candles on the blue frosted cake. "They're not in the house are they?"

"I forgot them outside," he said, running his finger along the base of the cake and scooping frosting from it. Mandy pushed him away.

"You better go put them in that old fish tank we got in the garage."

Chad opened the outside door to the driveway where he left the bucket of newts. They were all floating, some belly up, and when he touched the plastic bucket, he felt how warm it was from the sun radiating off the blacktop all day. He poked one of the lizards and it sank under the water and bobbed back up again without moving. He got a flashlight from the garage and took the bucket to the back yard where Mandy's garden lined the far fence. Lifting a large stone, he poured out a waterfall of the limp, red bodies into the cup of wet dirt the stone had sat in. The water filled the hole and sank into the earth, leaving the lizards piled on the dirt. The beam of light from the flashlight on their wet bodies made them look glossy and alive, but he placed the rock back into its hole and covered them. He put the bucket down next to the rock and walked back to the house.

There were no clouds so he could see several stars. Through the kitchen window he saw Mandy sitting in a chair next to Gill. Halfway across the lawn he stopped and heard her singing "Happy Birthday." He watched as she reached out with a lighter and lit each candle. The flames danced on the cake. Seeing the light on their faces he thought of all the days he'd missed, the things they'd done without him, and all the times he only wanted to be with them inside his own home. He felt each germ of human loneliness grappling up his sides. He looked up and understood why people used to chart monsters and gods in the stars, like Cassiopeia, or Orion, rising sideways and throwing a leg over the horizon. It wasn't just to move ships across the seas; it was so they could imagine something to compensate for the force of being pulled into the earth by the daily tasks of being human.

The next morning, Mandy went out by herself to run errands. Chad was in the den when he heard Gill wailing out in the back yard. He ran outside and saw Gill standing with the empty red bucket in his hands. Gill's face was blotchy from crying and Chad couldn't get him to stop screaming.

"I let 'em go, Gill. It's okay. I let 'em go," Chad said, reaching for the bucket from his son, but Gill pulled back like he were about to be hit and screamed louder. "Gill, it's okay. Let's go inside. Do you want some cake? You want some more birthday cake?"

Gill shrieked louder and looked around the yard like he expected to see the lizards bounding in different directions. Chad felt a tension mounting on his shoulder like a saddle from the screaming.

"Look at the birds, Gill. Look up there," Chad said, pointing above their heads where a small group of swallows shot across the sky like a wave of coal flecks on a twisting breeze.

Gill kept crying, but looked up at the birds until his bellowing fell in tune with his breathing. He pointed up to the drift of birds as they flew away and then pointed back down to the red bucket hanging from his other hand.

"We can't catch a bird with a bucket, Gill," Chad said, looking at his son, who immediately started screaming again.

"Okay, okay. You want to catch a bird? Is that what you want? Will that make you shut up?" He looked at the boy and back at the sky as a crow flew overhead.

Chad had taken sea survival classes to earn his Z-card. He had to spend half a week in a classroom learning about firefighting and ship safety, and half the week in a pool practicing with rescue rafts and float suits. A book he had to read described how you stay alive while adrift in a life raft with limited supplies on board. It had a description of how you can use fishing line to catch birds for food. There was a black and white drawing diagramming a sailor holding a seagull under his arm while twisting his torso like he were exercising until the bird's head tore away from the body. Chad recalled the stenciled sailor looking happy with himself despite being adrift.

Gill was still crying and pointing to his bucket, and Chad tried to remember how it was you caught a bird at sea, and how he could convert that to doing it in his back yard. "Okay, Gill. Okay, you want to catch a bird? Your dad will catch you a bird. Will you like me again if I do that?"

At sea he'd have to tie a floating lure to a fish line and pay it out away from the raft. Then use a second length of fish line with a slip knot floating in a wider circle around the lure. Then, if a bird came down after the lure, its beak would go under water from the force of its dive, and you'd pull the slip knot closed around its neck.

Gill sat against the fence with the red bucket in front of him. He was still crying but softer now, like he sensed something being done to fill his bucket. Chad straightened the hooks of three wire hangers and stuck them into the ground, end-to-end in the shape of a triangle. He rested the noose of the slipknot he'd tied into the fish line on top of the hangers so the knot was elevated. He went to the garden and lifted the rock he'd buried the newts under. They looked the same as they had last night but the rock had pushed their bodies into the mud. He peeled one of the small red bodies out of the dirt by the tail, and then looped the tail with a second strand of fishing line. He put the dead newt in the center of the hanger triangle and paid out the line to the edge of the yard where Gill sat. Both fish lines were in front of him as he sat next to Gill. He patted Gill on the knee, but Gill screeched and pulled away.

"It's okay, Gill. I'm sorry. It's okay." Gill sat back up and rested cross-legged next to his father. "Look at the newt," Chad said as he took one line in each hand and started pulling one slightly to shake the dead newt in the center of the lawn. Gill was still breathing heavy from his crying fit, but now stopped to watch the newt twitching on the end of the line. They sat in the yard side by side watching the newt, then the sky.

Chad didn't want to get up and go inside until Mandy came home and could pacify Gill if he started another fit. He sat next to him holding the spool of fishing line in his hands for over an hour and his legs became stiff. He ran his thumb over the line feeling how sturdy it was. He wanted to put an arm around Gill but feared he'd bellow bloody murder and the neighbors would call the police. He started thinking about what Mandy was doing. All he had wanted was to get home to her, and all she seemingly wanted to do was have some time to herself now there was someone else to watch Gill. He understood that, but sitting next to his son he thought that if being situated in a home life was once an ambition of his, it was a lonely man's naive ambition, and that no one could have expected something like this.

Gill grunted and then held his breath. Chad looked up and saw a hawk circle the lawn. The hawk circled again and dove straight into the center of the lawn. Chad stopped twitching the line with the newt on it. He grabbed the other line with both hands and as the hawk's wings hit the upper edge of the hangers, Chad pulled, cinching the knot around the bird's yellow-brown legs just above its talons. He stood up as the fine sheen of fishing line rose from his hands in a taught strain that cut upwards and through the air over him like a living kite rising and falling. The hawk's wings beat hard with a *thwack* each time they snapped shut. Its claws were clutching the small, red newt. Gill stood up next to his father as Chad lifted one hand over the other pulling in the line. Every foot he pulled the bird closer, it took a half-foot back. The line slipped over the palm of Chad's hand like he was a fisherman of birds of prey.

The fishing line that Chad had reeled in was falling in tangles at his feet, and Gill grabbed a coil of the loose line. Chad pulled until the hawk flapped wildly just over his head. Then the hawk let go of the newt and snatched at Chad's forearm, cutting the skin where its talons pinched down. He reached up and grabbed the bird's legs just above the talons and let it beat at him with its wings. He hooked a finger into the knot and loosened it until it slipped off, and only Gill and he were holding the fine line. Chad held the bird by the legs just in front of him until it stopped beating its wings and relaxed his grip. For a moment Chad held the wild bird and felt like he were Adam in the Garden, taking his first look at each new creature before voicing its new and eternal name. Chad felt Gill lean against him to look at the bird.

Gill still held the line that now connected only him and his father and stood admiring their fierce catch. The bird's eyes looked right at Chad like the dark globes were flashing some wild reverence to its captor.

"Jesus, Chad! What are you doing?" he heard Mandy exhale

from the driveway where she stood staring at him after dropping a large brown shopping bag.

"I don't know," he yelled back to her, lifting his arm and opening his palm. *Thhakk-thhakk,* the bird rose out of the yard and flew over the trees.

Gill was still leaning against his father and looking at the sky. Chad looked down at the cut on his forearm where blood was flowing out of the gash. He looked at Mandy again, who was pulling something out of her purse and running towards him. It looked like a small white flag, probably a handkerchief or napkin. Her arms were reaching for him, and her face looked concerned and wanting: wanting to love him, hold him, or mother him; wanting to clean off the blood, as it is the blood that counts, the blood that holds all things, and alone can pay the price of being part of a home.

He felt that perhaps now they could find a way to see things clear again, be together again, as this must be how people make it through year after year, always looking for ways to start again.

About the author:

After winning third prize in *Glimmer Train*'s Short Story Contest for New Writers in 2007, Devin Murphy has since had stories published in *Many Mountains Moving, R.kv.r.y Quarterly, Glossolalia*, and *303 Magazine*. He is currently an MFA student at Colorado State University. Prior to that, he spent three years working on expedition ships that traveled the globe.

JUNE AND STEVE
©2009 by Vickie Clasby

June occupied the gaily colored upholstered chair, holding a well-worn photo album in her lap. She carefully turned the pages, one by one, and her expression changed with each page. Memories passed through her consciousness like scenes from a black and white TV show. She moved her fingertips lightly over the worn photos, as if her touch could establish a connection with someone long gone.

Lost in her own world, she didn't notice when Steve claimed the matching chair next to her. He sat quietly, watching June, admiring her regal beauty which belied the years. She possessed a serenity he could never hope to have. He didn't know why, but suspected it resulted from the fairy tale life she'd led. She'd spoken often of her life with Ward and her two sons. The fairy tale ended after fifty-two years, when Ward succumbed to cancer. Steve knew the photo album she cradled kept those wonderful memories alive.

Suddenly, June glanced up at Steve. "Good morning, Mr. Douglas. How are you this fine morning?"

Her smile warmed his old heart. Just the sight of her took his breath, and he was momentarily speechless. He stalled for a moment by cleaning his glasses, pretending he just noticed her. "A gracious good morning to you, my dear. How did you sleep?"

"Quite well, thank you. I had a most wonderful dream." Remembering her manners, she added, "And how was your night?"

"I would love to say it was peaceful, but I'm afraid I tossed and turned. Just the usual aches and pains."

"I'm so sorry to hear that. Perhaps Dr. Allen can give you something to help you rest."

"Oh, enough about me. I appreciate your concern. But do tell me about your dream. It's sure to be more interesting than an old man's infirmities."

"Since you asked so kindly." June laid aside the photo album, and sat up straight in the padded chair. "It seemed like we were still in Mayfield, but it looked a lot like St. Louis where I grew up. You know how dreams are. Anyway, Ward was leaving for work. We lived in this wonderful house with a huge kitchen. I had just gotten a brand-new Frigidaire. Wallace and Theodore were going to be late for school, and I made pancakes for breakfast, and was afraid they weren't going to have time to eat them. Ward said he could take them to school so they wouldn't be late. He was wearing his brown suit. He just looked marvelous in that suit."

June had a faraway look in her eyes while she talked, like she was standing in that kitchen, wearing her apron and holding a spatula, and looking at Ward with doe eyes. Steve pictured her that way, just from hearing her description.

"Wallace sat down in the kitchen with his basketball under his arm and devoured those pancakes. Always had such a hearty appetite. He's a coach now in Michigan. I was the captain of my basketball team in high school, you know." She smiled, blushing slightly.

"Ward asked him where Theodore was, and Wallace just said, 'Gee, Dad, I don't know.' Ward went upstairs to get him, and he was still in bed. He had spots all over his face like chickenpox. It's funny I would dream that. Theodore never had chickenpox. It seems he'd drawn the spots on his face with one of my lipsticks. Ward and I couldn't help laughing at the lengths Beaver would go to, just to miss school. He was always getting into mischief. It's a wonder he made it through school at all. But he turned out just fine, has his own company in Scranton. Makes forklifts."

"So how did the dream end?" Steve didn't really want to know as much as he wanted her to keep talking. He loved her stories, even when repeated.

"I just woke up. It was so real, like it was happening right then. When I realized it was a dream, I was sad. Disappointed, I suppose. The dreams are when I'm happy, when things were like they used to be, when we were all together. Like these pictures."

Steve saw the joy leave her face, the spark in her eyes fade, replaced with the familiar look of someone who's lost what's most important. He reached out his hand, and she placed her delicate hand in his.

Steve's life had never been a fairy tale. Widowed with three sons, he'd accepted the loneliness as just a fact of life, until Barbara came along. She'd brought such joy into his life. Having a woman in his home changed everything. Uncle Charley had done a wonderful job keeping everything together, but a woman's touch was sorely needed. And when the boys all grew up and moved out, they still had Barbara's daughter, Dodie, to keep them young. But when they moved from Bryant Park to Cleveland so Barbara could take care of her dad, he felt like he'd lost his family, who were all back in California. Then Barbara died suddenly, and he was all alone.

Those years in Bryant Park had been such happy ones. Now there were only infrequent visits from his sons, his grandchildren, and *their* children. He didn't blame them. He knew it was hard to travel with a family halfway across the country. His health was too poor to travel anymore. All those years of smoking a pipe had ruined his lungs. He could barely breathe sometimes and only survived because of the excellent care he received here.

His mood now matched June's, so they sat there holding hands, together yet living in their respective pasts. After a half hour or so, an attendant approached June, placing a hand on her shoulder lightly to avoid startling her.

"Mrs. Cleaver, are you ready to go to the dining hall now?" She brought the wheelchair alongside the upholstered chair.

"Oh, my. Is it lunch time already?"

"Yes, ma'am. Salmon today. I know it's your favorite."

"Wonderful. The cook does a marvelous job with poached salmon."

The attendant helped June move from the plump chair to the rigid wheelchair, carefully transferring her withered legs, which had been useless for several years, but still sported fashionable shoes that matched June's tasteful outfit.

Steve struggled to stand, using the arms of the chair to brace himself. The thin tube at his nose snaked its way to the small tank attached to the aluminum walker. He breathed deeply, attempting to supply his tall frame with oxygen, yet felt little effect. He plodded along behind June's wheelchair to the dining hall where others awaited. Darrin Stevens, Ethel Mertz, Howard Sprague, Jane Hathaway, and Sam Drucker always sat together with Steve and June.

It just seemed they had a lot in common.

About the author:

Vickie Clasby resides in suburban splendor with her husband, thirteen-year-old daughter, eleven-year-old twin sons, two cats and a crazed Husky mix dog. She works as a business analyst for a major healthcare company. After completing a BA in English, she taught Freshmen Composition for what seemed like years but was in fact only months. Realizing she was not well suited for academic life, she worked at various jobs before returning to school, passing the CPA exam and beginning a career which does not embarrass her family, who hoped she'd get this writing thing out of her system. Her life is filled with corporate drama, domestic chaos, and endless writing material.

Vickie writes short stories, essays, and novels. She is a member of the Tennessee Writer's Alliance and the Williamson County Council for the Written Word. This is her second time as a finalist in the Scribes Valley Short Fiction Contest.

BETWEEN A ROCK AND A HARD PLACE
©2009 by Mimi Sharpe

In the summertime about five people a day ask me "how the hell" I live in the desert. They refer to a flat plain of black rock and boron beneath a brutal sun. My home is a tin coffin—*trailer* in city vernacular—on California's desert country, the land that flies out in unending monotony between Bakersfield and Needles; long, flat and moonscape. Every now and then there's a jutting palm tree, looking like something that fell from a nursery truck bound for Malibu. Mostly there are Yucca plants and green/brown twiglets that don't even have a name because no one cares what they are. Animals living in the desert stay underground during the day. Coyotes, prairie dogs, snakes and lizards. When we were kids my brother and I used to play with the lizards and prairie dogs, running after them, playing a kind of hide and seek.

These days the only time I see them is glancing off my bumper as I drive to and from my job at the local DQ/convenience store in Ludlow. I serve soft swirl ice cream, sell gas and give advice about the weather at Lake Havasu. Not that I ever go to the Lake myself. Pure tourista: full of jet skis, racing boats and people living on weekends with a vengeance. Families laced with plastic money and desperation for fun. They spend half their day traveling to the Lake, racing up and down it for two or three hours, piling all their crap back into their four-wheel-drive utility vehicles, and heading back to where they came from. Sometimes they talk my ear off about their boats, day, and lives; other times they just bitch at me 'cause their kids are crying or they maxed-out one of their credit cards.

Often enough, they ask me how I came to the desert. I usually give them an invented story about a poor sick father needing me to come home from the big city to care for him. But it's a complete lie. There is a reason, but I'm not sure I could ever explain it. As for my Dad, he's been dead eight years now. I got back to Ludlow (actually he was in a hospital in Barstow) two days before he died. I don't believe he ever knew I was there. By then my dad was a vacant body with tubes coming out of everywhere, all the humanity purged. Even his thick, calloused hands that had worked for years at the boron plant looked clean, frail and foreign. My brother sent flowers.

After Dad died, I drove back to the trailer to tie up loose ends. I called my brother to see if he'd be out for the funeral. He begged off, saying work was too heavy there for him to take the time to travel out for a funeral. He never even told me what type of work he was doing or whether he was married or not. It was a short phone call.

At the trailer, on top of Dad's console TV, there were old photos of my brother and me, stuffed into ill-fitting frames. An 8x10 of my mother hung by a piece of tape above Dad's bed. The photo was torn and frayed around the edges, as if it had been handled quite a bit. She looked to be about twenty years old, with her mahogany hair pulled up in combs at the sides, a shy smile wavering across her face. It bore no resemblance to the expression she wore the day she left: a smile that was caustic and bitter. It was the day after my sixteenth birthday; balloons still taped to the kitchen ceiling, leftover birthday cake in the fridge.

I can still see her tossing her beat-up, green Samsonite into the backseat of Aunt Jennie's car, slamming the passenger door. "Love doesn't grow on dirt and cactus, Lisa. You can tell your father that. Not a god-damned thing grows on dirt and cactus except more dirt and more cactus!"

I never told Dad what she'd said. He never asked. She ended up settling in Bakersfield, working as a clerk in a grocery store. After the divorce was final, Mom married a large, hunky, heavy-drinking construction worker named Don. Six months into the marriage, Don withdrew all the money in their checking account and skipped town with my Aunt Jennie. Mom eventually moved to Eureka; something about a job dispatching trucks. I got a few cards from her after that, saying how much she thought about us. She called me once on my twenty-third birthday, but she was drunk and crying, and most of the conversation had to do with people and places of which I had little or no knowledge.

After Dad died, I should have cleaned out the trailer, sold it and gone home to Sacramento, where I'd been living for the previous ten years. But I didn't. Instead I scoured the trailer top to bottom; sopping up pools of grease on the range top, scrubbing streaks of grime in the shower and washing off the thick film on the windows. Once it smelled clean enough, I moved in. Just for a while, I told myself, just till I stopped feeling sad, guilty or tired.

I hired a handyman to come out and paint the trailer its original colors of turquoise and white. I had a satellite dish installed so I could get more than one fuzzy channel and bought a new air conditioning unit. I even fashioned a rock garden in back of the trailer.

I called my boss in Sacramento and quit my job. I told him I was a "little lost" and having a "life crisis." People in California pretend to respect people who are lost or battling a crisis. They always mention "counseling" in the same manner a doctor might prescribe Tylenol with Codeine for a variety of physical pains.

Two of my coworkers called and asked after my "mental" fatigue. Ludlow, they'd explained, was not a place a person went back to, but they understood how a person could get lost, or depressed, or both. I told them I wasn't lost, I knew exactly where I was. Everyone in Ludlow knows where they are.

I took a job as an invoice clerk at a Barstow pallet plant. It was a long commute, but I never once thought of moving to Barstow. It looked too much like a micro-version of Sacramento.

On a broiling evening about a month after I'd started my new job, the eight-year-old Pontiac I drove died in the pallet company parking lot. There was a thick gray plume of smoke from the exhaust and a death rattle. A guy who worked in the warehouse offered me a ride home. He was a nice man, kind of quiet, shy smile, crinkly blue eyes. I'd noticed him in the office once in a while. He was always staring at his feet, with a kind look on his face.

"Whoooeee," he said as I poured him a cold drink at my trailer. "You live like a jack rabbit, right out here in the middle of nowhere."

Turned out, he was something of a mechanic and fixed my car for the appropriate compensation. Not, mind you, wholly monetary. He'd been watching me, he said, and he kind of liked jack rabbits.

"Sam" took to staying over with me a couple of nights a week. He didn't talk too much and was easy to be with. He fixed the plumbing and put in a new molded shower stall insert. He took to calling me "sweetcakes" and rearranged some large boulders in my rock garden. A few months passed and he told me I should move in with him. Not long after that he told me I'd be a fool not to marry him. For a quiet man he had loud ideas.

I let the twiglets with no name wind through my rock garden like long fingers. Grease pooled on my range top. Dust collected in the window sills. Most weekends I stayed with Sam in his Barstow apartment. Living things in Barstow came out in the daytime and stayed out at night. They made one hell of a ruckus. Especially Sam's little sister Alma. Alma hated Barstow. She hated the desert. She attended beauty school and fully intended to take off like a "big ass bird" the day she finally passed hair weaving and cellophaning. Alma said, often, that the only thing worse than living in Barstow was living in a trailer. She'd glance in my direction when she said this, as if gauging the impact. Sam thought Alma was spunky and had a "good head on her shoulders." He said he was too shy to live in the big city, but Alma was too full of life to live in the desert. I wasn't sure what Alma was full of, but she was as mean as catshit.

The day Alma graduated beauty school I told Sam I could not and would not marry him. We were sitting out on the patio of his apartment, watching a lizard stalk a fly. His normally calm, crinkly eyes glanced at me with a fire I hadn't seen before. Who the hell did I think he was? he wanted to know. What kind of fucking game was I playing, anyway? Why had I led him on? Sam wasn't going to be anybody's "damn fool." He stared at me with hurt, anger and dashed pride. I told him calmly that it was not my wish to make him a fool. I told him I hadn't been playing any kind of game and that I didn't know exactly why I couldn't marry him, I just couldn't. Maybe I didn't love him enough, I said. Maybe I couldn't love anyone. Maybe I hated Barstow. Maybe I just wasn't the marrying kind. I told him about my Mom running off. I told him I'd only heard from my brother once since I'd waved to him as he left on a Greyhound bus bound for points east some fifteen years before.

Sam said he wasn't interested in excuses or any of "that shit." He didn't see how any of it had anything to do with him. "You're a cold bitch," Sam said, tears welling in the corners of his crinkly eyes. "You pass through this place like one of those long trains that wind through the desert at night."

The following Monday I quit my job at the pallet factory. I didn't give a reason. I sat in my trailer for two weeks, eating everything I had in the house. I didn't answer the phone. Sam drove out to the trailer a few times. I refused to answer the door. The last time he drove up, he stood outside the trailer with his tanned, work-worn hands on his hips, yelling, "You think there's always going to be someone wanting you? Not out here, lady. All there is out here is desert. Just desert and heat and little animals that hide in the daytime. Don't worry 'bout me, though, 'cause I'll do just fine. I'm a good man with a good heart and I don't have to hide from anyone."

I almost yelled back at him that I didn't give a good god-damn whether he had a good heart or not, that people with good hearts didn't force other people to see things their way. But it was 120 degrees that day. Too hot for a living thing to argue. Time for living things to be inside or underground. I watched him walk back to his truck and drive away. He didn't look shy anymore, he didn't smile. I never saw him again.

A week later I grew tired of watching forty-two channels and starving. I drove out to the DQ five miles from my home and had a hot fudge sundae. I noticed a Help Wanted sign in the window and applied. I've been working at the DQ ever since. I cleaned up the trailer and weeded out the rock garden. If there's anything that needs fixing these days, I do it myself. When people ask me much of anything personal anymore, I just lie to them. It's easier that way.

Everyone passing through Ludlow is going someplace or coming back from someplace. A few are lost or meandering. Some of them are brash city people who lack patience and are filled with arrogance. Some are tired or sick. Some are hot and bored. Once in a while someone comes in with a shy, wavering smile like the one my mother wears eternally in the photograph above my bed. Sometimes when they return, coming back from where ever they went, they look tired and worn. They live above ground both day and night. It is hot, tiring work.

By day I give out gas, ice cream and information on the weather to people who drive too fast to notice the black stone and boron. They only feel the heat. They bring the heat and the exhaustion in with them to swirl around me even in air conditioning. I'm thankful when the sun sinks below the flat plane of my vision and the day closes. I'm prone to talking to myself as I count out the day's receipts and lock up the food counter.

When I get home in the late evening, eyes peer at me from behind yucca plants and unnamed twiglets, black like the night around us. The eyes scare city people and folks with frantic expectations. They don't scare me. I see better in the dark. The eyes comfort me, give me scale and perspective. Before I pack into the trailer and settle myself down to watching forty-two channels, I walk around to the Rock Garden in the back and stand very still in the dark. I once caught a coyote tumbling a couple rocks in my garden. I swung the beam from my flashlight in his direction and caught the side of his face as he glanced back, running. His head was lowered, but I could clearly see a shy smile, full of need and exhaustion moving fast along the ground, away from the trailer and Ludlow.

About the author:

Mimi Sharpe was born in Syracuse, New York, lived in Kansas for a time during childhood, and settled in Northern California since 1961. After graduation from high school in 1970 she attended Ohlone College in Fremont and later attended business school in Hayward and the Academy of Art in San Francisco.

She has always been artistic and worked as a freelance artist for some years, focusing on pen and ink and oil pastels. She's had a few gallery showings in the Bay Area. She moved to Sacramento in 1977 and has loved it there ever since! A beautiful river city with lovely landscapes and wonderful people.

Mimi has been writing creatively since she was eight years old—poetry and short stories. Though she still pursues her art and continues to write poetry and short stories, she has worked as an executive assistant for a lobbying organization for all the cities in California since 1985.

She has been married for 25 years and has a 23-year-old daughter who is currently attending college at Sacramento State University. In addition to drawing and writing, Mimi enjoys cycling, singing, and reading. She's known in her family as the "literary snob" due to a distinct bias toward 19th century English literature. But she loves to read both fiction and nonfiction (mostly politics, history and philosophy).

She is rarely seen without a book in her hand. During the time she was raising her daughter, she stopped writing, but now has more than enough time to dedicate to that activity.

Her favorite authors are George Eliot, Thomas Hardy, Anthony Trollope, E.L. Doctorow and Richard Russo. Her favorite short story writer is Alice Munro.

MARIA'S GIFT
©2009 by Hannah Greer

What I'm about to write happened thirty years ago, but I remember every detail as if it were yesterday. Some will say it is nothing but a tall tale, a crazy woman's embellishments of past experiences that occurred more in her dreams than in reality. The truth is, each of you can take it the way you wish, but no one will ever wrench from my heart and soul the conviction that a dying old woman living in the midst of Anasazi country in the heart of Mesa Verde gave me a gift that would change my life forever.

It was a typically hot, dry August that summer in Mesa Verde, a beautiful national park situated near Four Corners—aptly named for the geographic connection of Colorado, New Mexico, Arizona, and Utah. As an anthropology enthusiast and history teacher, I was eager to discover as much as possible about the Native American societies that had dwelled in the area for over 1,000 years. There was a strong spiritual aura about the region that chilled my bones and sent pin-pricks traveling up and down my spine. Coming upon the bend in the mountainous road leading up to Mesa Verde, I stopped to gaze at the most remarkable site: the Cliff Palace composed entirely of sandy bricks crafted by the Anasazi and nestled entirely in the palm of a menacing precipice across the wide expanse of valley 10,000 feet below. Even from a distance, the energy of the dwelling permeated my soul.

"Who were you, Anasazi chiefs? Why this place? Who were you hiding from?" I had a million questions. Some were easily answered by the pamphlets I had received before beginning my summer trip. The Anasazi were a mysterious tribe of Native Americans who were believed to inhabit Mesa Verde beginning around 780 A.D. The name translates "The People," but I connoted it to mean "the chosen ones."

The Mesa Verde area held true to its Spanish name meaning "Green Table." It was blessed with rich soil conducive for growing the staple maize. But, why farm on top of the canyon and live in treacherous cliffs below? Perhaps the Anasazi were peace-loving, god-fearing people who just wanted to be left alone. They chose isolation from other tribes known to hunt and kill.

"Why Four Corners?" I wondered. What I discovered next would convince me that this was no ordinary place to be sure. This was truly sacred ground.

Entering Mesa Verde was a spiritual experience in itself. There was something totally peaceful and mysterious about standing on the now barren table which masked the existence of entire villages hundreds of feet below. To tour the dwellings, a traveler must climb down narrow ladders barely visible to the naked eye. It is believed the Anasazi used hemp ropes to gain access to the treacherous, concealed entries.

Bear in mind, reader, that visitors brave enough to look southward see nothing but precarious rocky precipices leading down to the bottom of the valley. I heeded the tour guide's advice to look up or straight ahead to keep from hyperventilating. I'm glad I did.

The true wonder occurred when I jumped from the ladder onto the tightly packed red earthen entrance to the cliff palace. I couldn't help but gasp at the beautiful, natural architecture before me. The Anaszai mastered building one apartment atop another over a thousand years ago. I highly doubt present-day abodes will endure the ravages of time, even two-hundred years from now. As I stood in awe of the amazing structural design, the wind swept through the small windows and doorways the ancient architects placed throughout their dwellings, creating a refreshing breeze and incredible ventilation system. The sounds, however, played tricks on my eardrums. I believed I could hear the people chanting methodically, adding lyrics to nature's beautiful melody.

Walking inside one of the rooms in the Palace, the voices from the past encapsulated every part of me. Although I could not understand the language, I could comprehend the messages of peace and prosperity. These were a people who cherished family and demanded a respect for nature. Nothing was to be used up without good reason and without replenishing what had been borrowed from Mother Earth.

In order to prepare for harsh winters, the Anasazi knew how to provide for times when food would not be plentiful. Each condo had an attic space carved out of solid rock. When the first excavations occurred on the area, perfectly preserved kernels of maize were discovered in each one of these ancient silos. I could smell the sweet scent of the maize as I continued walking through the structures.

Cliff Palace consists of 150 rooms. As daughters married, they went to live with their husbands' families. The men would add on additional rooms for the new branches of the clan. As I moved toward the center of the Palace, the chanting became stronger. I wondered if anyone else had heard the epiphany, but no matter, I knew I did. In the center of the dwellings stood the spiritual room, a *kiva*, where the clan practiced democracy to perfection. Family members met regularly, sitting in the circular structure so that no person held superiority over another. Anthropologists believe that all major ceremonies occurred in the *kiva* including weddings, births, and deaths. The village's sacred secrets passed from one generation to the next and the keepers of these confidential oral enigmas were sworn to secrecy, never to divulge them to any outsider. It is one of these ancient practices that affected my life from that moment on.

Being peaceful people who lived off the fertile land, the Anasazi spent much time developing crafts. It is believed they discovered a way to create black pottery naturally, not dyed or burnt. This earthenware bore its raven hue all the way through the piece, and no one could discover how the feat was managed. Most of the artifacts crafted had something to do with familial customs: wedding vases with double handles signifying the joining of a man and woman; stoneware nesting bowls symbolizing the development of the child from infancy to adulthood; and a large variety of figurines, each with a special power to help clan members who were ill, anguished, depressed, or infertile. Now you might wonder why any Anasazi would have reason to be depressed? Well, their world was not without its dangers. Hundreds of baby skeletons were found on the bottom of the canyon floors. It appeared that toddlers often overstepped the boundaries of the cliff dwellings and fell to their premature deaths. The loss of each precious offspring was mourned, and prayers for new souls to replace the lost loved ones abounded. Fertility sculptures, made with love and hope, were carefully worshipped in the *kiva* and given to the mourning couple to assist in creating a new life.

How I became the recipient of one of these fertility structures and how it changed my life is what I've been coming to since I began this tale. Heading up to the gift shop on top of the mesa after the cliff dwelling tour was an adventure in itself. The young sales clerks spoke perfect English and added much new information about their people.

I was mesmerized by the tiny ebony clay figurines on one of the shelves. One of the sales clerks noticed my unmitigated interest in the small clay gods. This twenty-ish young woman, Miakoda, was eager to explain the different black clay figurines to me. Taking down the array of birds, foxes, wolves, fish, turtles, and bears—she gave a detailed account describing the utility of each one. I demonstrated particular interest in a tiny bear, no bigger than the width of my dainty palm. Miakoda carefully reached for the bear and placed it snugly in my hands. I felt the energy of her ancestors emanating from the girl's flesh as our hands touched for a fraction of a moment in the exchange of the precious figurine. But it is what she related to me that sent shivering sensations down my spine:

"The little bear...it is for you. You must keep it close to your heart. You will see in time. Things will change. There will be children in your life. What once did not reap a harvest will soon enough. Please, it is fine Santa Claran pottery...its value is precious but its powers are more. Believe me."

My head was spinning. How could she know? One reason I took this trip was to forget the pain of the previous year. My husband and I successfully conceived a child that died in the womb. I've not been able to conceive since, not even with endless, tortuous fertility procedures. We wanted children so badly, and the barrenness in my womb filled me with a dark despair. Traveling through Native American territory was an attempt on my part to become one with nature; to see the world through people who successfully lived in harmony with Mother Earth. Regardless of my thoughts and my past, I had not mentioned any of these torments to Miakoda, so how did she know I was infertile? I asked and she skirted an answer:

"My people know many things. Your eyes tell me your sadness as they longingly watch our children play. Your hands tremble with the loss. Your voice sings the sad song of barrenness. Let me help you. Do as I say. Go visit the wise ones and you will know the truth."

Again, the girl covered my hands with hers so that we both gently but securely smothered the black bear in my palms. Perhaps I was overcome with emotion, but I tell you that the little object warmed in my hands. I could almost feel it move of its own accord. Recovering from my shock I whispered to Miakoda, "Where are these wise ones?"

"They are on your journey. You go to Arizona next, am I right?" she asked.

"Yes, to the Hopi reservation. I believe the Anasazi were their ancestors, right?"

"Yes, that is true. The great one, Maria, is the elder who holds the secret of the black clay. She is dying now, but she still appears from her home on the reservation at the new moon. It is said she has taught her daughter the old secret. These people, they will have more information for you. Take this bear and go. The spirits of my ancestors are with you."

I wanted to pay for the bear, but Miakoda would not take a penny. She told me that I had come to Mesa Verde for a reason and her ancestors wanted to make this gift to me. I asked her how she knew I was going to Arizona next, but the girl smiled and diverted her ebony eyes from my gaze. I thought it would be rude for me to continue an interrogation, so I accepted my little treasure, hugged my new acquaintance, and left the shop.

Once I was back in my hotel room, I examined the bear from top to bottom. It looked almost primitive—a simple body ending in two pointy ears at the top; loosely defined appendages; a tiny bump where the snout protruded; and pin-prick eyes and nostrils. Wanting to ascertain the secret of the black clay, I carefully scratched at the material, hoping that I would not discern the creature was a sham. I was not disappointed...the bear was truly black through and through. Its shiny exterior felt good in my hands, and I began to think of my new possession as a talisman. I cradled it in my arms and chanted my own prayer to the Anasazi, to God, even to my ancestors. I wanted a family more than anything in the world. I was only somewhat surprised to discover I had drenched the little bear with my bitter tears. I had come to forget what had happened, but I discovered the pain had followed me to this sacred place.

I christened the bear Ana, in honor of the Anasazi, and she traveled in my shirt pocket to the Hopi Indian Reservation in Arizona. It didn't take me long to discover which house was the famous artisan's. Maria was well known for her craft and many of her pieces sold for thousands of dollars. Her people told me she no longer received visitors, but that she would rock on her porch occasionally, so if I kept a daily surveillance, I might spy her. That is all I needed to hear. I parked a decent distance from her front door each morning, hoping for a glimpse. I sat for hours, holding Ana in my palms and praying.

On the seventh day of my vigil, the door to Maria's house creaked open. The morning sun drenched the porch in a maize-colored light. A young girl walked towards my car. I knew she was much too youthful to be the matriarch I came to meet, but perhaps she was a younger version of the old woman. The girl tapped lightly on my car window and I rolled it down. She introduced herself and gave me a message from her grandmother, Maria:

"My name is Mary, after my grandmother. She is very sick and told me to tell you she is sorry she cannot meet you. She wanted me to say that life is not always easy. Sometimes that which we want the most escapes us. But the human heart is strong and powerful; the soul has magic that can communicate with those we love in the spirit world. Sometimes a special gift from a stranger who feels another's deep pain can help ease the wounds and aid the healing. The bear sprang from the inner ground, where the soil is enriched by the blood, the toil, and the tears of those who have come before. The blackness of the bear represents the sadness it has pulled out of the earth. It holds the sorrow so that you may find happiness where now there is an absence of optimism. Your home will be blessed with children. And your children's children will multiply by two to make up for your loss. Be strong and do not lose hope. Return to your husband knowing that your life will change."

At the end of her speech, Mary performed the same ritual that Miakoda had. She cupped my hands in hers, the little bear embedded between my flesh and Mary's. Again, I felt the heat emanating from the figure's interior, infusing my blood with a healing warmth and energy. Mary added some words in her native tongue and kissed me on the cheek. I felt like I had been caressed by an angel.

A gargantuan weight lifted from my heart, and the months of endless torment and agony subsided. I didn't quite understand what had occurred in this unique region of the United States or why I had been chosen by The People as a lonely traveler in need of their healing medicine. A selfish part of me didn't want to know for fear that I would be forced to relinquish this gift of expectation. I decided to accept what I had been given and to keep the prize a secret, my method of carrying on the Anasazi's tradition of protecting the ancient ways. The rest of the journey was uneventful and I returned to my husband to begin the rest of my life.

I told you when I began this tale that many of you would not believe what I present. That is for each of you to decide, but the story won't be finished until I relate what occurred after my Mesa Verde experiences. I purchased other black pottery pieces before going home, so my husband never thought too much about the little bear that I kept on the nightstand next to our bed. After a few months with no child on the way, I began to believe I had been duped. But just in case my analyses were incorrect, I continued my prayers and kept positive thoughts in my private conversations with Ana the bear.

My husband and I also began to seek out adoption agencies to improve on our chances of having a family. The social workers were reticent to give us a hopeful outlook about ever adopting a baby. Ana and I continued our nightly rituals.

A few months later, we received a call about a teenager, due in about a week, who wanted to give up her baby. A few days later, we were blessed with our miracle baby—a little girl who was a smorgasbord of genetics: Irish, German, Scottish, and Native American. It was the Indian ancestry that caught my attention. Within a year, we had been offered fourteen babies, all from the southwest. We did not provide a home for each one, but we did become the parents of a darling baby boy who was about a year younger than our daughter. Was this Ana's doing? Our family was surely multiplying.

Our daughter was perfect with her red hair, brown eyes, freckles, and olive complexion. Her high cheekbones added to her beauty. As she grew, she developed a keen interest in horses and nature. By the time she was five years old, she was riding like a professional. The child seemed to have a special gift with animals. She was continuously moving injured animals she found into her makeshift veterinary hospital. In addition, she was a wonderful artist who liked using natural substances for her crafts. She especially loved working with clay, and one piece she crafted in particular almost made my heart stop beating. Our daughter created a clay sculpture of two brown hands cupping the world, with a tiny black bear sitting on top of Mother Earth.

Our son became the spokesperson for every misunderstood child in his school. People loved his quick wit, his peaceful manners, and his devotion to fighting for the underdog. He was a man of the Earth and friend to all its creatures. Our little boy's black hair and dark eyes reminded me of Miakoda and Mary. Not only did his features resemble these incredible matriarchs but also the cadence of his voice echoed the melodic chanting of the spirits in The Cliff Palace. He could tell a great story and captivated other children with his accounts of historic figures that made this country great.

My husband and I were truly blessed. Fearing something dreadful would happen, I continued to thank Maria, Mary, and Miakoda through my conversations with Ana every night. The bear's surface lost some of its natural sheen from years of being held and rubbed. But she withstood lots of hard knocks provided by our darling toddlers who seemed mesmerized by this little black bear. I never told them the significance of the fertility goddess, but I did say that she was a gift from some very special friends I met a long time ago. There were times I thought I was truly hallucinating, for Ana's eyes seemed to sparkle whenever my children spoke to her.

When our daughter was about six years old, I had a dream. Ana spoke to me in perfect English, telling me that part of the gift had been fulfilled but another remained. The next generation would multiply in twos to make up for my fertility problems. I wrestled with the temptation to relate my imaginings to my husband and children. Ultimately, I decided to keep the prophecies to myself and to patiently wait and see what transpired in the future. Shortly thereafter, I found it difficult to keep my pledge.

One morning, while I was combing my daughter's silky, straight hair, a thought pulsated into my conscious mind and would not release its grip on my soul. My little girl was holding a doll and a horse, pretending the baby was her child. As I finished braiding her long hair, I blurted out for no apparent reason, "Someday when you're a grown-up woman you are going to marry. And you and your husband are going to have twins!"

She giggled at this news. "Twins! Yuck! Mommy, if I have twins you can keep them for me until they're grown up! I don't want to clean up after them. I want to ride horses! And boys are nasty! I'm never going to get married!"

With that she skipped out of the room, and the subjects of marriage and family rarely emerged in our conversations. The years passed by so quickly, it was hard to imagine that our babies had become adults. Our daughter met a wonderful man who also happened to be part Native American. He too adored the outdoors and riding horses. After a long courtship they married, and several years later, they became parents of a beautiful set of twins, a boy and a girl. My grandchildren received the best features of their parents: honey-colored red highlighted hair, green eyes, high cheekbones, and olive complexions.

When the twins were a few weeks old, my daughter broached the subject of the divination I related to her many years ago. Although I could not provide a rational explanation for the forecast given to me by Mary and Maria, I successfully convinced her that some miracles should not be excessively scrutinized. She has become less cynical about the powers of hope and ancestral love over time. My son, a devout believer in the supernatural powers that bless humans, is convinced that his children will also come in multiples.

I leave it to each of you to decipher my tale to your own liking. As for me, I am grateful every day for Maria's gift. My grandchildren look at me with knowing eyes, as if the ethereal powers of their ancestors blessed me with their omnipotent gifts. As I write these words Ana sits by my side waiting for me to go through the daily ritual of caressing her ebony body and whispering, "Thank you, my dear Anasazi friends. Thank you for the best gifts I have ever received."

About the author:

Hannah Greer has embraced writing since she was a child. As an educator and founder of an experiential school, she guided underachievers to utilize their imaginations. Seven years ago she co-founded Chrysalis Experiential Academy, Inc. in Roswell, Georgia. The students have written anthologies of their writing every year and the school has produced many budding authors. Community members are encouraged to submit their art and stories, as well, and two of the anthologies have been published in both English and Spanish. Hannah loves to write.

WOMAN TO WOMAN
©2009 by Atossa Shafaie

Roxanna pulled into the safest spot she could find. She was certain she was in the wrong place. The Motel 8 sign shed a neon reflection flickering with a lonely buzz. She dug into her bag, sifting through her court ID, cigarettes, loose change, and the book she never got to read, until she found the index card with an address scribbled on it.

"12664 West Washington Boulevard, room nineteen," she confirmed. "This would be it."

Roxanna examined herself in the rearview mirror. The curse of beautiful green eyes was non-existent lashes and pale brows. As a young girl born in Persia, her fair complexion won Roxanna the rank of outcast among her peers. Years later, when she traveled to America to study, her exotic combination was considered intoxicating. She much preferred American tastes, even now. Thankfully, dim lighting made it easy to ignore new lines tiptoeing down any corners. Straight hair, still warm from her hairdresser's blow dry, was a new shade of auburn. She popped open her dark brown lip gloss. In mid-application, her cell phone started ringing Blondie's "Call Me" and she jumped.

With subconscious ease, her hair tossed in synch with the cell phone flip, "Hello?"

It was her husband Ali, and he was not happy.

"What? I'm busy," she snapped.

That did not make him happier.

"I told you I'm working late tonight. There are seven new cases on my desk, and I have to hear them first thing in the morning. You're her father, figure it out yourself."

Ali was flustered because he didn't know what Arya was supposed to have for a snack before she went to bed. Arya, of course, knew exactly what she wanted. Her little six-year-old voice plucked instructions in the background as Ali was trying to talk.

Roxanna couldn't tell him where she was. Haleh was banned, and Ali very strict about it. They were happier now. Roxanna had waited a long time to have her husband back, to no longer be wife number one out of two, but just wife. Iran remained a memory curled deep under piles of rubble, not to be disturbed.

Haleh had been silent for two months. Why did she have to call? She expected what, exactly? Roxanna put the car in reverse. *What the hell am I supposed to do?* She asked herself. *He wouldn't take Haleh back anyway. Not after that business with the language instructor.* She shut her eyes and breathed deep, putting the car back into park. A strange pitch in Haleh's voice on the phone resonated the undetectable key of last chances; undetectable unless one knew exactly where to look.

The fog was dark but it was lifting. The glass in Roxanna's hand was empty again. Her face stuck to the cold tile floor. Thick velvet curtains kept out anything fresh. She laughed to herself. There was a bottle of Vodka waiting for her, even in revolutionary Iran. But she would have to get up, walk through the living, to get to it. Step by step the movement outside would be a new summons, but she was still in mourning. She curled her knees to her and wrapped herself in a false blanket of lost things.

Women can't be judges, the new power said, not even lawyers. Go home, they advised with a hiss of accusation, and be a wife to your husband, a mother to your children. They could not know, of course, and she would never tell. Ali had once confessed, just before their first kiss, that he didn't want children. If any part of her had been unsure, those words seduced her. Three years later, when they were wed, he promised her coming back home would be the last thing he ever asked of her, and she was lured. The law, in post monarchical Iran, decreed that before a second wife was had, the first must consent.

Roxanna's mouth stuck to itself, begging for the bitter sting of anything numbing, but she could tell Haleh was in the garden, playing with the damned birds. Wife number two, favored by all, and herself almost a child. Better stay still. The room was not cooperating. Sliding between sleep and nausea she passed what must have been hours.

Roxanna suddenly felt small hands guiding her to sit. Her head pretended to be a carnival ride, and she crumpled over. Haleh helped her up again. Roxanna's joints creaked, and, somehow, that slight young girl held her weight as they shuffled somewhere. Fresh air smacked her skin, and she shut her eyes as natural light forced itself on her. Roxanna sat on a stone bench. From above, cages creaked delicately in the breeze. The birds inside sang a nauseating, sweet melody.

"See," Haleh said. "Some of us who are caged can still find music."

With a weightless love, Haleh opened one of the cage doors. A small canary hopped out onto her finger. "She has learned to tell fortunes, this one," Haleh cooed proudly. She took a small box full of folded papers and put it in front of her canary. It cocked its head to the side, chirped, and hopped onto the box. With a blank stare, it poked a sharp beak through the jumble and picked out a fortune carefully, fluttering back onto Haleh's finger and trading the paper for a small piece of fig.

"Do you want to know what it says?"

Roxanna wanted to go back inside. Haleh unfolded the paper.

"In the hope of union, my very life I'll give up. As a bird of Paradise, this worldly trap I will hop," she read with a crystal laugh.

Hafiz, Roxanna thought. How fitting. Roxanna sat in the garden, and allowed the girl to bring her tea, let the birds sing their songs. She didn't drink the tea, or hear the sounds, but the fog was leaving, and she was letting it go.

Roxanna wrapped manicured hands around the steering wheel, resting her forehead on them. Her three-carat diamond dug itself into her skin. Hopping out, she activated the alarm, deactivated it to be sure it had worked, and reactivated it again.

Room number nineteen was on the second floor. She grabbed her purse close to her chest and peered into dark corners in front of her. Her daily hour at the gym allowed for a doe-like sprint up the unlit staircase. Nineteen, nineteen, she went the wrong way twice before she finally found it. The door was cracked.

"Haleh?" she asked. "It's me."

There was no answer. There was no light either.

"Haleh?"

She felt along the wall until she found a switch. The dingy room looked untouched. Dripping water tapped evenly from somewhere in the back. A musty smell crept past her into clean night air. On the orange comforter of the bed closest to the door, a black chador[i] was neatly folded. Haleh's family's Qur'an[ii] was beside it, a stark white envelope perched on top. Roxanna's name was written on the front, in Haleh's handwriting. A tendril of alarm stretched awake, reaching up Roxanna's spine for the hairs on her neck. She sat on the bed, and with shaking hands, opened the envelope.

I hope this ends things between us. What it begins for you I cannot say. I miss Iran. I miss my garden. It was your garden once, wasn't it? I actually felt sorry for you then. It was my duty, as second wife, to bear his children and help you prepare his home. But you showed no interest in him, or me. I was relieved that you stayed out of my way. But I see now that if you could have given him Arya, he would never have come looking for me. You should know I tried to make him put you aside, but he would not. You should know that. Ali promised me a garden here. Los Angeles doesn't have gardens. I wonder if he knew that. I suppose you are stronger than I am. You would never do this. You left your life in America to come home to Iran with Ali. And you made a new life there. Before the revolution, you were a judge. I *was so scared of you, an Iranian woman judge. And when the Mullahs came, you survived them. And when Ali told you he wanted me, you survived us both. They don't have good pomegranate in California. Ali promised me they would, but it isn't the same. I remember, as a child, running through the summer orchards. The fruit was round and plump and redder than anything I'd ever seen. Here, the fruit has no character. I don't have a home anymore do I? After this, my father will not have a daughter named Haleh. What does he need with his youngest, when he has two upstanding elder daughters to be proud of? But tell him I remember, I remember everything he taught me. I am no longer a Muslim. But, I am still his daughter. When he can stomach it, ask him to think of me. As for Ali, tell him that I am sorry. Ask him to forgive. I should have done as he wanted, and taken off my Hijabⁱⁱⁱ. Walked in the sunshine with my hair free. But I could not. I should have honored my husband and told anyone who rose a brow that I was your sister. I should have stayed quiet when Ali took you to the courts to adopt my Arya. He was right to do it. Without you, our daughter would have been a bastard with no place. Everyone has to have a place. I should have done many things differently. But I could not. I could not. Tell him that I never meant to betray him. That the longer I stayed here, the more I lost, and to my worthless shame another man's trickery found me. A man who did not look around the room at anything but me. A man who seemed to me so beautiful and young compared to my stern Ali, almost my father's age. He promised things that he never meant to. Now, I am left. Tell him that I know what a foolish thing I have been. Tell Ali that my being his wife and Arya's mother were the sweetest things in my life. I know that hurts you, but you have them both now. Please, tell him. There is one last thing between us. You will be Arya's mother, and I am glad. You will see that she is strong and she will find happiness. But teach her, please, help her to remember who I am. Ali will want her to forget, and I don't blame him. But I ask you, woman to woman, to whisper in her* *ear when he is not looking. Whisper that her mother loved her, even as she left. Either way, whether you do these things or not, for me, it is finished. The rest is yours.*

I am a daughter of Allah, and by his will, may he forgive my crime against him.

Haleh Robadi Aryanpur

Roxanna couldn't breathe. She crumpled the paper in a balled fist and looked around the room waiting for some sign of what to do next. Her heart paced angrily, wishing to be free of her ribcage. A damp *pat, pat, pat* reached her throbbing ears. She looked to the direction of the sound.

On shaky legs, Roxanna walked to the bathroom. She turned the knob, opened the door, and fell to her knees. Haleh's thick curtain of carbon hair fanned weightless atop a sheet of cooled water. Her emptied eyes stared straight ahead. Sliced wrists bobbed up and down in a brimming tub. The round swell of a newly growing stomach broke the water's surface.

Roxanna screamed. She crawled to the bathtub. Pulling herself up, she put one hand on Haleh's pregnant belly, the other on her own barren womb. Her wedding band glimmered where droplets touched it. Through wasted tears she wondered who was to blame. It was then, among the steamy pitch of moist air, that she saw herself in the mirror, dripping, disappearing under a film of mist. She sat on the toilet, hugging the crumpled letter to her chest. Rocking back and forth, she willed her body to get up, call someone. But the letter was a weight she could not lift.

Suddenly, wings fluttered above Roxanna's head, infusing stagnant air. One of Haleh's canaries perched above the bathroom door, preening citrus feathers. Roxanna's eyes shrank from the bright plumes. Looking away, she saw Haleh. Hidden beneath the lifeless face lurked a reflection of the little girl who at this very moment was wrapped up in bed listening to her father read her favorite story.

Roxanna dropped on all fours. She began to mop up the floor with almost white towels. Thickened water inched through her pants, staining her pale skin. What the hell was she going to tell Arya? What was she going to tell Ali? She scrubbed harder, her hair curling as it clung to her face, beads of sweat dripping off her forehead. When she had no more towels left, she threw them in a pile under the sink.

"God damn it!" she screamed. Someone walking by outside paused, and Roxanna stopped breathing. Motionless, she prayed for the stranger to walk on. When they did so, she quickly ran to the door and bolted it shut. She then drained the tub and wrapped Haleh in her Hejab as best she could, making sure to cover her face.

With the bird's cage set on the gate open, Roxanna waited. The bird finally hopped in, as Roxanna knew it would. Cross legged, on the soiled Motel 8 bathroom floor, she pulled the birdcage closer. The dripping water mercilessly kept its pace and Roxanna shut her eyes, head cradled in her hands. The bird started singing. Chaste chords seemed full of hope and Roxanna recalled the syrup scent of Haleh's roses. Velvet blooms had come to life under her young enthusiasm, bursting where once only weeds could grow. That garden had always belonged to Haleh.

Blondie chimed a muffled "Call Me" from her purse. Roxanna edged a laugh. She rose and pulled herself together. She wiped the mirror with her sleeve, and tried to remove the streaks of makeup marking her tear-stained face. Roxanna stole one last touch of the wet, stunted life beneath the black robe stuck to Haleh's limbs. She kissed the abandoned girl limply on her forehead. Roxanna left the Motel with Haleh's bird, her letter, and her Koran, which would be given to Arya when the time was right. *Arya,* she thought, and began to walk faster, breaking into a run. She needed to get home and hold her daughter before she fell asleep.

[i] An outer garment worn by some Iranian women when they venture out into public; it is one possible way in which a Muslim woman may follow the Islamic ḥijāb dress code A chador is a full-length semi-circle of fabric open down the front. It is thrown over the head and held shut in front. A chador has no hand openings or closures but is held shut by the hands or teeth or by wrapping the ends around the waist.

[ii] The central religious text of Islam

[iii] The Arabic term for "cover" (noun), based on the root حجب meaning "to veil, to cover (verb), to screen, to shelter"

About the author:

Atossa Shafaie was born in Tehran, Iran. The revolution caused her family to move to London, England and then to the United States. She has a B.A in English Literature from George Washington University and is currently working on her first manuscript entitled *Blood of Persia*, historical fiction about Cyrus the Great, founder of the Persian Empire.

THE DECORATOR
©2009 by Melissa Tantaquidgeon Zobel

Everyone loves the gray goddesses of Mystic, Connecticut, USA. These fearless old women let their gray braids flap in the wind as they bike across town or fiercely kayak down the winding Mystic River. They buy organic grains at the Pilgrim Health Food Store, decorate their homes with shells and sea glass, and receive regular supernatural guidance from the most senior goddesses, who live in the old part of town. All of the local thirty-something women dream of the day their first gray hair paves the way for admission to this coven of contemporary good witches.

Wanda Stark never forgot the year that she joined the group. At fifty-two, her shoulder-length ashen locks took on that enviable oyster glow and her interior design company, Stark Interiors, won second place in the Connecticut Design Awards. She was proudly poised to become Mystic's preeminent gray goddess, until the "For Sale" sign came down in front of the tumbledown Victorian next door. When a friend at Cove Realty revealed who had purchased it, Wanda downed the bottle of L'Esprit Cognac that had come with her second-place design trophy.

Wanda's new neighbor was none other than Zola Black, the internationally renowned Queen of Interior Design. Wanda had spent her entire life imitating Zola. Now, with the real McCoy next door, she suddenly felt like a Canal Street knock-off camped out on Madison Avenue.

To make matters worse, Zola was also the world's penultimate gray goddess. *Mystic Lights* newspaper joked that she had moved to town simply because Mystic was "the only place on earth where she could become truly invisible." Yes, when Zola went biking, her famous locks would simply melt into the sea of silver braids that flapped down River Road, and no one would even blink an eye.

Still, it was impossible for the creator of the planet's most beloved line of earth-friendly home furnishings to truly vanish. Her organic designs flourished from Tuvalu to Times Square. In Greenwich, Connecticut, the group fondly known as "Greener Witches" erected a statue of Zola Black right beside "Girl Standing in Nature," for her shocking conversion of several prominent Stepfords into heartfelt tree-huggers.

Zola's creations even lured Upper East Side clients with sumptuous labels, like "White Tiger's Last Kiss," penned to a sleek line of black and white faux fur furniture, and "Dear Rafflesia," a three-dimensional wallpaper that appeared to be woven from the actual petals of its gigantic floral namesake. Her designs were so natural-looking that some suspected Zola of having cut an unholy deal with Mother Nature herself.

However, Zola Black had worked hard to find inspiration, globetrotting to places like Chaxa Lagoon, just to glimpse a coral flamingo, or Madagascar, for a peek at a golden-eyed lemur.

Yet, right now, there was not a single exotic trip scheduled on Zola's Blackberry. She had deleted them all. Her only immediate plans were nursing an adorable Somali kitten and re-decorating a monstrous Victorian mansion in New English Mystic, right next door to Wanda Stark's perky little ivory Cape Cod.

Zola's publicist, Formaggio, spun the tale of her move from Manhattan to Mystic as "A great lady's decision to grow old gracefully by the sea." Wanda knew that was complete horseshit. He had obviously googled "Mystic," found the world-famous Mystic Seaport, and neglected to check its location on the map. In point of fact, Zola's new home was nestled into a marshy elbow on the Mystic River, a serene tidal estuary that spilled gently into Long Island Sound—which was still a good long ways away from the Great Salt Sea. If "life by the sea" was what Zola had really wanted, she could have easily settled down a dozen miles to the east, in Watch Hill, Rhode Island, where the great stone mansions stick their sturdy necks out into the open Atlantic and thumb their noses at each passing hurricane.

No, this "life by the sea" shtick was simply a watery ruse. Something was up. Somewhere in Zola's musty celebrity closet, there was a sordid tale of tax evasion, recovering substance abuse, forbidden liaison, or some other equally spicy peccadillo. Wanda felt sure that the scandal of it all would come out eventually. But for the time being, she chose denial: Wanda would simply pretend that Zola Black was not really there.

Today, the commuter train back from Grand Central Station had left Wanda too hungry, sooty, and oxygen-starved to think straight. She lay, crucifixion-style, on her couch until a timid knock signaled the arrival of the garlic-scented goth pizza delivery boy. Surprisingly, the door opened onto a blast of patchouli, wafting from a shiny silver ponytail clipped with a Celtic knot barrette. This sweetly-scented visitor donned a powder blue LL Bean fleece and was demurely cradling a small plant with baby pink blossoms. Although Wanda was still armored from head to toe in stolid New York black, she could not make a single drop of conversation flow in the direction of that powder blue fleece.

It did not matter. The woman seemed perfectly comfortable handling all the introductions herself. "I'm Zola Black," she extended a very small hand. "And you must be Wanda Stark. Having a decorator as a neighbor was quite a selling point for me. No worries about inflatable Christmas decorations or plastic lawn critters next door, if you know what I mean."

Zola pressed the potted plant into Wanda, whose hands remained frozen at her sides. "This foxglove is for you. Someone sent it to me as a housewarming. But I have a brown thumb these days, and your garden is so beautiful that I thought I'd best turn it over to you." A downy auburn kitten popped out of Zola's fleece pocket. "See what I mean?" she chuckled. "I almost forgot to feed my baby." She scratched under the kitty's tiny chin. "This is Russ.

He's a ruddy Somali, though you can't really tell yet. He'll lighten up soon to his full russet glory." Zola's eyes glistened, "Wait till you see him then. He's a designer's delight!"

Wanda petted Russ obligatorily and hoped that Zola did not notice the bust of Brahms atop her piano. He was her favorite composer, more for his habit of shooting neighborhood cats, than for his music. Wanda was the only gray goddess in town without great tufts of cat hair stuck to her couch.

The angel inside Wanda's head struggled to compliment Zola on her stunning kitty and career, but the pitchfork-toting varmint won out. "So, what brings you to our fair little town?" she asked, with a sharply raised eyebrow.

Zola stiffened a bit, "I have never re-decorated an entire place, just for myself, and I thought it was time for me to find an old house by the sea and settle down."

Wanda gulped back the word "bullshit." She had seen that exact quote in a Zola spread in *Interior Design* magazine and it had made her molars hurt. "Well, I certainly look forward to the privilege of having a front row seat as yet another glorious Zola Black ecodesign blooms right next door."

Zola burst back emphatically, "Oh, no! Not at all, Wanda dear!" Her face twisted like a reflection in one of those carnival mirrors. "I have recently seen the light. I now understand the wisdom in the great Mr. Loudon's theories. I am sure that you hated studying him back in Architectural History class. We all did, back in our design school days. But what fools we were! I finally understand him now. I no longer find my inspiration solely in nature, but from man. I want this house, my Magnum Opus, to clearly reflect the beauty of being human."

The woman, whose signature style reflected an erotic love of Gaia, was suddenly glorifying man! It was all crystal clear now: Zola Black had suffered an irrevocable breakdown. It was only a matter of time before the tabloids caught on and camped out in Wanda's shrubbery.

The phone rang and Wanda seized the opportunity to politely

blow air kisses and break free. Unfortunately, her escape from insanity was only temporary. On the other end of the receiver was a hysterically shrieking woman, whom she readily determined to be her sister, Sandra Stark O'Connor.

"For God's sake, Wanda!" Sandy shouted. "Please say she's with you! I've called everyone else! Please tell me Moira is at your house! She is there? Isn't she?"

"No, Sandy" answered Wanda, hollowly. "What's wrong?"

Sandy spoke between choking sobs, "I went to school...today...to pick her up...and there was no sign of her...anywhere."

Wanda wished that she felt more surprised. Moira O'Connor was the kind of child you worried about constantly, even when you were standing right next to her. Similar-looking children, with red hair and green eyes, were a dime a dozen in Mystic. But Moira O'Connor was hard to ignore anywhere. Her red locks were not the usual carrot, auburn, or strawberry blond. They carried flecks of fire and flowed like molten lava down her back. Neither were her eyes a normal shade of green. They were paler even than the lime-colored lichen on river rocks.

Oddly enough, Sandy never thought much about her daughter's looks. She reminded her too much of her husband Clancy. However, the old-timers at the Mystic Irish-American Club claimed that Moira O'Connor was a throwback to something far stranger than ole Clancy. They said that she was kin to the ancient wee folk of the Emerald Isle. Clancy scoffed at that malarkey and insisted that the O'Connors of County Cork had looked the same for generations. Moira O'Connor was simply daddy's little girl.

However, daddy had not been around to see his little girl lately, having run off after a tussle with her mother three weeks ago. When Sandy told the police about their domestic squabble, the officers winked at one another warily. Mystic folks were skeptical of anyone who could lose both a spouse and a daughter in a matter of weeks. People in this whitewashed colonial village usually kept better track of one another than that.

At Sandy's house, Wanda scanned the Internet for inspiring stories about children who were found safe after kidnappings. Elizabeth Smart. Delimar Vera. Natascha Kampusch. Kerstin Fritzl. Yes, they were all saved.

But there wasn't always a happy ending.

On day five, the neighbors stopped bringing potluck casseroles to the O'Connor home, and after one full week had passed, the police recalled their officers from the case to investigate a fire at the Flannery Brewery.

It wasn't callousness. If the truth be told, everyone just figured that Clancy did it. Yes, Moira O'Connor was surely safe somewhere with her father. Clancy was renowned for being both irresponsible and intentionally cruel.

After another full week had passed with no new clues as to Moira's whereabouts, Wanda decided that it was time to kiss her lifeless sister goodbye and head back home to pursue her own crumbling life's journey.

As she passed Zola's place, she observed her rival gleefully mix paint, slap it onto the wall, then shake her silver head in disgust. Wanda sighed. At least the old grand broad still mixed her own colors.

On the thirteenth day after Moira's disappearance, four of Stark Interiors' biggest clients fell away. After all, Mystic was a hive. Any weird organic soda, unusual fisherman's catch, exotic scone recipe, or new-internationally-renowned-designer was snapped up for group consumption within a matter of weeks.

Nevertheless, gray goddesses tend to be optimistic folk. So Wanda Stark did not contact May Apple, the infamous local herbalist, for something to end it all. Instead, she logged into her Web account and cashed in a modest portion of her 401K. After all, Zola was supposed to be "simply growing old gracefully by the sea" and she showed no sign of actually setting up shop. So there was no need for alarm.

In the days to come, Wanda carried on as usual, taking her old Scott bike out for daily spins on the river, right past Zola's house.

On the fifteenth day after Moira's disappearance, Wanda bent her wheel by peddling straight into an old granite hitching post with the following sign attached:

OPEN HOUSE SATURDAY
1 Room Ready for Viewing!
Complementary Pumpkin Pecan Pie and Hot Mulled Cider
Black Designs, *Now Accepting Local Clients*

Clearly, the four horsemen of the apocalypse had arrived: Her niece had been kidnapped by her father, her clients were falling away, her fabulous 401K was shrinking, and the country's leading designer was now accepting clients right next door!

Unfortunately, Wanda was not the only one who passed Zola's house that day. By Saturday morning, the Mystic Yacht Club was filled to overflowing with folks who had sailed in from all over just to trample Wanda's backyard ferns en route to Zola's opening. Armed with her own personal invitation (stuffed under her door by Zola on the morning of the event), Wanda skipped the lengthy queue and tapped boldly on the front door. The Grand Gray Goddess herself answered and wrapped Wanda's arm around her own. Then, she loudly proclaimed what an honor it was to have such a tremendous local talent be the first to see her work. Wanda could not stop beaming until she entered the newly designed dining room.

"I call it Mystic Picnic," Zola purred.

Wanda Stark's heart began to bleed. The barely-peach walls seemed to melt into the honey oak flooring. Overhead, plaster reliefs of laughing sailors danced around an "upside down wedding cake" chandelier made of sunlit smoky quartz crystals that speckled the walls in such a way that they appeared to be dripping with hot cocoa. Beneath the chandelier, a cherry dining room table was polished to a radiant crimson gloss and set with plates which featured whaling ships bathed in peach, cherry, cocoa and mint pastels. The floor-to-ceiling toile curtains featured a scull race between the two bridges of the Mystic River, as observed by picnicking spectators in similar candy-colored hues.

The old Zola Black would have themed her design after Mystic's gray-green river reeds, sparkling midnight blue waters, and soft russet ospreys. Those old designs inspired folks to send money to Al Gore and recycle their laundry detergent bottles. But Zola's new view of the world was more like *Alice's Adventures in Wonderland*. People were deliciously silly, confectionary creatures in a luscious realm of purely human design.

As Zola put it (in the origami flyers which had been artfully strewn all over the house), "It takes real inspiration to design a room that reflects the beauty of human beings. I thank the people of Mystic for giving me that inspiration."

Even now, Wanda refused to fully panic. But she did make a formal list of her options:

Retrain as a tour guide at Mystic Seaport
Study to become a blackjack dealer at the Mohegan Indian Casino
Take up fortune telling in the old part of town

Unable to settle on any one option, she went online to gut what remained of her 401K.

The next day, Wanda was washing down a cold slice of clam pizza with a frosty bottle of Stella Artois when a knock came at the door. She was so startled that she peed herself a little and guzzled the Stella before answering.

Sure enough, it was the devil herself, and Wanda could think of nothing to say but, "Would you like to join me for beer and pizza?"

What happened next over Belgian ale and clams was all make-pretend, or so Wanda thought, until she sobered up enough the next morning to read the contract slipped under her door. Zola had offered Wanda a fifty-fifty partnership! She claimed that she needed a partner to avoid so many solo trips to New York City and to gain an insider's eye on local color. Wanda's lawyer naturally rushed through the paperwork, but he did warn her that Zola would likely be declared incompetent for making such a ludicrous offer.

While the two designers were meeting to sign the final contract, Wanda received a call from Sandy saying that Clancy had deposited fifty thousand dollars into her bank account without explanation. When Wanda told Zola, she asked her what sort of person steals his own child and then sends money. Wanda responded that such a question was rhetorical if you knew Clancy.

Two months after Moira O'Connor went missing, another open house sign went up at Zola Black's house:

"Come for Chowder in our New Kitchen!"
Black and Stark
Now Accepting Clients

The new partnership's name made everyone chuckle. Black's claim to fame was her bold application of every color in the rainbow, whereas Stark's palate ran the full spectrum from Ivory to True White. Surprisingly, their new kitchen suffered from neither extreme. Black quartz countertops contrasted with olive stained cupboards set against a rustic parchment wallcovering which featured historic herbalists like Tamsin Blight, Old Mother Clutterbuck, and Marie Laveau, alongside their exotic remedies. The central dinette portion of the room was constructed from two old Congregationalist pews beside a table made from a glass-topped colonial door with Holy Lord hinges. On a shelf above, an antique stoneware salt jar was surrounded with several bundles of garlic, over which sat a tea cup rack painted with the tasseographic topics of *Amore, Soldi, Corsa, Famiglia, Lavoro, e Spirito* (Love, Money, Travel, Family, Work, and Spirit).

To maximize the mystical effect, they added hand-blown glass drop lights, which cast an otherworldly violet haze on everything, including the black kettle of chowda on the stove. Stark and Black aptly dubbed this room, "Mystic Cauldron." Such a funky design would never bring them acclaim among the Silk Stocking crowd, but it would surely make them truly beloved with the Aran sweater and Docksider set in Mystic, Connecticut.

The two gray goddesses were dressed in hand-woven linen jumpers, and their hair was loosely swooped up with hand-forged copper barrettes. As they greeted visitors, they were radiant, until they came upon poor Sandy O'Connor, wearing a yellow ribbon on her sleeve.

"You didn't have to come," insisted Wanda, shame-faced.

Sandy was obviously trying very hard not to cry, and she hugged her sister limply. "I wanted to let you know that I was glad that you didn't cancel your big event simply because of the new developments."

"What new developments?" Wanda had not read a newspaper in weeks, nor had she checked her phone messages for the last day or so.

"You actually don't know?" Sandy whispered. "Another girl is missing. Her name is Carrie Mancini. You may remember her from Moira's birthday party last year. She was Moira's best friend. Clancy once told me that Moira said she could not bear living without Carrie. She and Clancy were both such drama queens. Two peas in a pod." She started to sob. "While the police were looking for Carrie, they found one of Moira's shoes in a sewer culvert. I've had to get a restraining order to keep the Mancinis from harassing me. They think my marital problems caused their daughter's abduction."

This was the worst, greatest day of Wanda Stark's life.

The next morning over Sumatra coffee, Zola wound her hair into a beaded Native American scrunchy and carefully read Wanda the following headline from *Mystic Lights* newspaper: "STILL NO SIGN OF CARRIE."

Zola popped up her head. "You know what?" she said. "I have a New York detective friend named Manny Spellman who might be willing to advise them." Zola shook her head in disgust. "I'm ashamed I didn't think of it before!"

At the Mystic Police Station, the sunburned locals all wore khaki shorts and faded baseball caps. The moment they saw Zola, they removed them and stood up straight, but Zola paid no attention, plowing straight through to the Police Chief's office. While she hooked him up with her New York cop buddy, Wanda poured over the corkboard pictures of her niece and Carrie Mancini. Yes, she remembered Carrie now! She had a mysterious smile, blue-black ringlets and violet eyes. A similar-looking older woman was talking to one of the detectives and the woman shot Wanda an accusatory look.

When Zola was finished, Wanda told her that she wanted to go home and have a good cry. Zola, for her part, said the whole thing made her want to go throw up. Around three a.m. that night, Wanda gave up trying to drink herself to sleep and turned on the TV. Noticing that several lights were still on at Zola's house, she took out her binoculars. It was hard to see much of anything through the heavy linen curtains, but she did make out two shadows moving back and forth.

If the truth be told, this was not the first time Wanda's binoculars had roamed across Zola's house. After all, Zola was an international celebrity who worked with Wanda every day, but shared nothing of her personal life. It was only by googling the latest blogs that Wanda discovered Zola was romantically linked to a Manhattan veterinarian, *and* that this new liaison was upsetting her long-standing relationship with an aging Italian painter.

Wanda caught another glimpse of the two shadows moving together and wondered whether Dr. Doolittle or Michelangelo had dropped by for a visit.

The next day at work, Zola was flushed and bursting with energetic, new ideas for the parlor. Meanwhile, Wanda was tired, hung-over, and not in the mood. So, Zola told her to take the day off and get some rest while she ran into the city alone.

This offer made no sense at all. Zola had made it crystal clear that she hated going into Manhattan alone, so Wanda felt well within her rights to pose several prying questions.

"Taking the cat to the vet?" she asked. "Looking for some new Italian art?"

But her prying only prompted a soft purr from her partner.

After Zola left for the train, Wanda gave in to her worst addiction. No, it was not the drinking. Drinking was the least of her worries. She could dry out from the booze for months at a time. No, Wanda had a darker habit, one that she could not break, not even for a single week: Wanda Stark was an incurable snoop. She had been in therapy for years trying to address this behavior but to no avail.

Her inability to resist "the need to know" was why she always wound up alone. It was not that she lacked adequate good looks, talent, or affection. Her last lover had bailed simply because he discovered that she hacked into all of his emails and financial records.

Wanda had tried everything: narcotics, aromatherapy, acupuncture, you name it. But the withdrawal from snooping always triggered a suicidal depression. At the moment, self-preservation meant prying open Zola Black's rickety back door. Once inside, the silence made her shiver. She had expected to hear Russ the cat squeal the moment she stepped inside.

Perhaps Zola had really taken him to see the vet!

The hallway was as they had left it, littered with paint cans and rows of design boards covered with samples of fabric, wallpaper, tiles, trim, and photographs. She waded through it all to mount the heavy staircase. Upstairs, Zola's room was easy to locate, as it was the only one with a bed—and a simple, no-frills, all-white, single bed it was at that. Wanda chuckled to herself about how much it resembled her own. Save the stunning Queen Anne desk and Steuben lamp, its freshly plastered white walls and institutional-looking bed made this room look like an asylum. Adding to the nuthouse mood was a ruddy paint sample slapped against one wall, which could have easily been mistaken for some bloody patient mishap.

Wanda gasped at what she saw next. Atop the Queen Anne desk sat two empty bottles of Silvertone permanent hair coloring, labeled with the caption "become a gray goddess." Wanda giggled with unimaginable glee and instinctively petted her own natural gray locks with newfound appreciation. Her snooping had already been rewarded with solid gold, and she had not yet even poked into Zola's desk.

There, she found a legal file stuffed with a pile of correspondence. Skimming for the juicy parts, one line instantly caught her eye, "Your tiger poaching and plant smuggling will not go un-prosecuted unless you meet our demands.' Imagine what fun the press will have when they find out." The letter was postmarked four months earlier from Malaysia.

Wanda could read no further. A flood of tears raced down her cheeks.

Could this be true?

What else could Zola be up to?

She rifled through another file labeled *Mystical Inspirations*. Inside was a photo CD. As she turned on Zola's laptop and tried to hack in, a veil of tears slowed her down.

Was Zola going to New York to pick up some new endangered animal from one of those exotic pet dealers as her muse for some new design?

Wanda finally gave up on hacking into the computer and searched the desk for a print version of the photos. Sure enough, a set of five-by-eight pictures was tucked in the same drawer. They depicted scenes of Mystic bikers, kayakers, tourists, a peregrine falcon, and someone who looked a lot like Carrie Mancini.

Then came the *thump*.

Zola must have forgotten something and come back home! Wanda stuffed the pictures back into the envelope and tiptoed into the next room. There was no overhead lighting, and this room did not even have a lamp. In fact, it was completely bare except for an elegant Honduran mahogany armoire. A second thump made Wanda choke, as it seemed to come from right inside the armoire. Wanda drew an angry breath and imagined that this phony gray goddess had trapped some poor peregrine falcon inside the armoire. As she turned the skeleton key to its lock, Wanda felt that she would surely faint. She cracked open the creaky door and listened hard for any pecking or scratching. Hearing none, she flung it open and jumped back. Two glowing eyes glared at her. She took out her cell phone and cautiously aimed its illumination at them.

There sat a small boy, gagged with a scarf and bound to a chair with tasseled curtain tiebacks. A long chestnut braid of hair lay on his lap. Several rosy paint samples were brushed on his face, and they nearly matched his lips. He was dressed in a Mohegan Pow Wow T-shirt, with a tear that exposed a patch of bronze flesh, and pinned to his sleeve were several bronze paint chips.

Wanda ungagged the boy and helped him into the bathroom for a drink of water. Leaning over the sink, he sputtered out something that sounded like, "I'm Parlor, I'm Parlor!"

"I'm Wanda, I'm Wanda," she offered, as he hastily gulped down several cupped handfuls of water.

"I know," he spoke hoarsely. "I have been listening to you for a couple of days. When I recognized your footsteps, I made as much noise as I could. I was just helping my cousin park cars at our Pow Wow, when your friend asked me for a hand with her bags. Then next thing I knew, I found myself being dragged around here to watch her decorate. The rest of the time, she locked me in the closet."

Wanda could hardly breathe. "I'm so sorry, Parlor," she said.

"My name's Sam!"

"I thought you said your name was Parlor," she said incredulously.

The boy groaned in frustration and dragged her downstairs.

"What's going on here?" she asked as he pulled her along.

"I'll show you." He threw open the kitchen broom closet and retrieved a Tupperware bin. It was stuffed with a bloody scalp of black curly hair and a violet paint swatch.

He tapped a knuckle on a hollow-sounding section of the recently sheet-rocked and wallpapered walls and said, "Carrie was 'the kitchen.'"

The black granite countertops, bathed in violet light, suddenly made Wanda swoon.

The boy imitated Zola's New York accent, "It takes real inspiration to design a room that reflects the beauty of human beings."

Wanda dropped the Tupperware onto the kitchen floor.

Sam pointed across the hall. Tacked onto the parlor wall were several swatches of bronze curtain trim, rose velvet fabric, and a chestnut paint chip. "I was going to be the parlor." He pointed to the old lathing, much of which had newly been torn away.

Blood raged through Wanda's fair temples as Sam dragged her into the next room.

"This house is a graveyard! We have to get you out of here, right now!" she choked.

"One more thing." He patted her fair, freckled cheek, and then pointed to the dining room's cocoa-speckled peach walls and pastel whaling ships. Wanda tried to pull away, but he drew her past the cherry red table to the toile curtains, where he pointed to a very specific spot.

Suddenly, Wanda wanted to shave every gray hair off her head and jump off the Watch Hill rocks, straight into the deep, blue sea. Among the picnickers along the Mystic riverbank, was a freckled, flaming redheaded child with green eyes paler than lichen, and seated beside her was a man who looked just like her.

Wanda froze for only a second before taking out her cell phone and dialing.

"Mystic Lights Newspaper," a receptionist answered perkily.

"Th-thank God it's you, Lena," said Wanda, her voice quavering. "I have some grave news for the coven."

"You're in luck," said the receptionist. "Our new High Priestess has not left yet for her meeting with High Priest Spellman in New York. I'll go and grab her."

"No! No! Wait!" begged Wanda, but the woman had clearly stepped away from the phone.

"Ms. Black," the receptionist called out, "you have a phone call."

About the author:

Melissa Tantaquidgeon Zobel is the recently appointed Medicine Woman of the Mohegan Indian Tribe. The former Medicine Woman, Dr. Gladys Tantaquidgeon, passed away in 2005 at the age of 106. Gladys trained Melissa in tribal oral tradition, and spiritual beliefs. After receiving a B.S.F.S. in history/diplomacy from Georgetown University in 1982 and an M.A. in history from the University of Connecticut in 1984, Melissa traveled throughout New England as a storyteller for the Tribe. She also served as Vice Chair of the Mohegan Tribal Council in the mid-1980s and a member of the Council of Elders in the 1990s. Since the mid-1990s she has been heavily involved in cultural themeing and design work for Mohegan Sun Casino.

She has written several books, including *Medicine Trail: The Life and Lessons of Gladys Tantaquidgeon* (University of Arizona Press, 2000) and *Oracles: A Novel* (University of New Mexico Press, 2004). In 1992, she received the Native Writer's First Book Award for a tribal history titled *The Lasting of the Mohegans*, and in 2002, she won an Emmy for her work on the historical documentary, *The Mark of Uncas*.

Melissa is currently employed as the Executive Director of the Mohegan Tribe's Cultural and Community Programs Department. Her department operates the Tantaquidgeon Indian Museum, the oldest Indian owned and operated museum in the United States of America.

Melissa and her husband, Randy, live in Old mystic, Connecticut. They have five children: Rachel, Madeline, David Uncas Sayet, Kaitlyn, and Emily Zobel. Emily is the youngest and she provided the inspiration for this short story.

THE FUNERAL DINNER
©2009 by Terry Dickinson

"They're with Jesus now," Karl's voice rasped as he laid a single red rose on each casket. He'd been crying silently for some time now.

Tim nodded. He didn't like that about himself: appearing to agree when he didn't. Not wanting conflict. He understood the religion; he had grown up with it. He knew the words, the hymns, the favorite Bible verses that supported the beliefs; he knew it all, but he didn't believe it, not any more. He had even spent over a decade of his working life in the pulpit. But that was all behind him.

Tim's slide away from religion was not the result of something traumatic, nor did it happen quickly. He guessed that he always had had questions but he never let them surface, never gave them a voice. Maybe it was part of a mid-life crisis. Maybe it was a confrontation with his own reality, discovering who and what he really was, admitting what he had never admitted to anyone, especially to himself.

It probably was unusual that the source of his growing atheism was not some scientific, anti-god literature, but the Bible itself. Tim had been preparing a talk to support the idea of Intelligent Design. He had always felt that the first chapter of Genesis paralleled the theory of evolution except that it involved a creator. For some reason that he couldn't put his finger on then, and couldn't understand even now, he saw something that he had never noticed before. How many times had he read that scripture? How many sermons had he heard and given from that text? Why had he never noticed?

But there it was. God created plants before He created the sun. Without the sun, the earth would have had no orbit, no season, and no source of heat. If it happened that way, the earth would have been a frozen ball of ice hurling across space. It didn't make sense. God—if there was a God—would be smarter than that. Plants before the sun is neither very intelligent nor is it a good design.

He canceled his speaking engagement. Said he wasn't feeling well. No, he would rather not reschedule. That was the beginning of the thread that led to the unraveling of his entire belief system. It was painful, and sometimes he refused to think about it.

But over the next several years he poured over familiar biblical stories and, in every case, he found that any story that appeared more than once contained unexplainable and self-conflicting details. Every time! He had been told—hell, he himself had said on more than one occasion—that the Bible was God's Word, perfect and without error. But the more closely he studied it, the more errors he found. Stories about the Hebrews in the wilderness, stories about the birth of Jesus, stories about the crucifixion and resurrection, stories about Saint Paul, stories about Judas, all disagreed in the details. And the disagreements couldn't be reconciled.

Once the Bible began to unravel, so did the culture. He became more sensitive to the hate and anger that lay hidden just beneath a varnish of love. He began to sense that the slogan "love the sinner, but hate the sin" was a hoax with hate winning nearly every time. He began to understand that trying to make converts was an act of superiority. He slowly realized that the talk about family values was code for the suppression of women.

The further he moved away from his childhood teachings the more hypocritical religion loomed. Only one thing continued to bother Tim—he was never able to share his thoughts and feelings with the people closest to him, his mom and dad and brother. He, for reasons he couldn't understand himself, needed their approval. He remained silent and pretended that he was still on the same page with them. Nothing could have been further from the truth.

"It was a good service," Karl's voice was stronger now. "We'll see you back at the church hall," then added, "Drive carefully. This ice is terrible, and I wouldn't want anything to happen to my favorite brother." Tim watched silently as Karl and Norma Jean walked to their car.

The funeral service had been of no comfort to Tim. It all seemed so mindless, so simple and gullible. The preacher talked as if he actually knew God, as if they regularly had morning coffee at the corner diner. God thinks...God feels...God wants...God says.... How does *he* know? Because he imagines it so? Because several thousand years ago someone who believed the earth was flat imagined it so? The funeral talk was all about God and very little about Mom and Dad. But Tim's anger was not about this funeral, not about this preacher. It was, instead, about himself. How many times had he used loss and grief as a tool to prod the vulnerable toward faith? How many times had he assumed that his own thoughts and attitudes were inspired directly from God? How many times had he ignored the complexity, beauty and frailty, and failures of the deceased, and further ignored the deep and necessary grief of the family to try to make a convert?

Back then, Tim believed that the end justified the means, that one convert was worth whatever it took, and the raw emotions at a funeral were pure gold.

But today Tim had wanted to stand up and tell everybody who his parents really were. That they were deeper than these simplistic notions about God. They were real, complex, struggling human beings who had their own fears and doubts and failures. Human stuff that they could never wrestle with because they had to believe—or pretend to believe—so others would believe and, subsequently, never be free to wrestle with their own fears, doubts, and failures.

Of course, there was no mention of the human struggles. That would imply that salvation could be earned. No one wanted to hear about Dad kissing his new bride goodbye and hitch-hiking two hundred miles in a January snow storm with only a light jacket and loafers to get his first job. Or that he had to borrow a nickel to put in the pay phone to call back to find out he had been hired. Nor did they seem to want to know about Mom's courage and strength raising two boys under the age of four and keeping the farm and feeding the livestock while Dad was half way round the world in a war.

They didn't want to believe that these were real people washed in their own blood, redeemed by their own crucifixions and resurrections. Instead, this funeral and these people seemed satisfied to talk about Jesus and heaven and faith and how we will all meet again on the other side if we accept Him as our personal savior.

Throughout the funeral sermon, Tim bit down hard on his rage until his jaw knotted and his graying beard bristled.

He waited for the others to leave and he stood alone and silent as the caskets were lowered into the cold, damp earth. First Mom's, then Dad's. He wanted to be alone. He wanted to take the time to get past his rage and allow his grief to surface. The soggy, gray clouds seemed to hurry past the treetops, all wrapped up in themselves as if they, too, were trying to escape the freezing rain that had been falling all day. Tim turned up the collar of his coat and stood with his back to the storm. Deep inside his head, anger and anguish collided like ice-covered limbs of the maple trees driven by a bitter November wind.

Tim walked slowly to his car, the brittle, icy grass sounding like crushed potato chips under his feet. He was dreading the funeral dinner. Most of his relatives were believers. He glanced back at the now-empty cemetery and felt a dull thud in his gut as the backhoe began filling the graves.

The storm was not letting up. The spruce trees that separated the highway from the cemetery were laden with ice and stooped like tired old men burdened with unforgiven regrets. Some tree limbs had already snapped under the load. Fortunately, the road crew had salted the main roads. It was slow going, but Tim was in no hurry.

As he nosed his PT Cruiser out of the cemetery and onto the highway, his mind drifted back to the early days. His dad had never encouraged Tim to go into the ministry, not openly or directly, but he beamed proudly when Tim graduated from seminary. Fifteen years later, when Tim resigned what appeared to be a successful and growing church, his dad was noticeably disappointed. They never talked about it much. The reasons Tim had given at the time were shallow, but his father had not questioned him further. He could never have talked with his father about the agonizing questions that haunted him, about what was really going on.

When he had resigned, he had been honest enough with his Board of Trustees to tell them that he had nothing left to say, that he had run out of words and needed time to re-examine his soul. That very day, when he walked out of the church, he had gone directly to the art supply store and bought new professional brushes. Tim had been interested in art since he was a child. In the middle of his third grade, when the old calendar was taken down, Tim had rescued it from the wastebasket and over the next several months, carefully drew portraits of each of the presidents pictured along the edge.

But there were no art classes in the schools in rural northern Michigan. It was just something that he enjoyed doing. However, as he sat alone and absorbed with his drawings, he would sometimes be interrupted by his mother insisting that he go outdoors and play softball with the neighborhood kids. They needed one more player to complete the teams and Tim needed the fresh air and exercise. This may have been the beginning of Tim's learning that the needs of others were more important that his own. What talent he may have had would not be developed until he signed up for a watercolor class at the local community college as an adult.

His greatest struggle in painting was no different than his struggles with his family, the need to please others. More recently he had begun to paint like he wanted to paint without looking over his shoulder for approval. His brush strokes were more certain and he was less inclined to blend his colors but rather let each color stand next to the other with opposing opinions and a bold assertion of their right to be; reds against greens, purple with yellow. The hues and values held hands like pieces of a puzzle that left the painting more mysterious and able to invite the imagination of the viewer into a dialogue to complete the work.

Now his art was beginning to attract some attention.

He stomped the mud and ice from his shoes as he approached the entrance to the social hall of the church. Tim knew what was about to happen and he dreaded it. They would talk about Jesus and their self-conflicting beliefs as if it were above question, and Tim would listen and nod politely and say nothing to point out the obvious contradictions. The relationship is more important than the ideology he would tell himself again. That's how he had gotten along with his parents.

As Tim removed his coat in the foyer low voices droned through the closed doors and engulfed him like a plague of locusts. The hum of the conversation was frequently punctuated with a "Praise the Lord" said with conviction and certainty.

Mom would like this. For her, everything was about God. It was God's mercy that Tim survived colon cancer—had nothing to do with surgery or radiation or chemotherapy—God's will! Praise the Lord! Never mind the question of where was God when he got cancer in the first place? But it was Mom and it was OK.

On a few occasions, not more than three times at most, when she and Tim were alone and honest, when Dad was not around, she would ask questions about faith and God and pain and suffering and death. Tim cherished those moments, those memories; they were real and honest and naked, without trying to cover anything up. Praising God was a way of putting the questions back in the closet. But here, for Tim, at the entrance to the funeral dinner, listening to the rise and fall of conversations, "Praise the Lord" was like fingernails on a chalkboard.

"You finally got here." Karl greeted him when he entered the hall. "We were starting to get a little worried. Hey, grab a plate and join us, we're over there," pointing toward the middle of the room. Karl was nearly three years younger than Tim but had lost most of his hair. He shaved what little he had left. At six foot four inches he stood nearly ten inches taller than Tim and had been an outstanding football player in college until he injured his back. He was still muscular even as he approached retirement age.

Tim liked his brother in spite of the frequent exchange of bloody noses in middle school when Karl started his adolescent growth spurt and left Tim behind. Through high school Tim answered to "Shorty." Tim's thick, curly hair was now his unspoken revenge.

Tim found an empty chair across from Norma Jean and sat down. Norma Jean didn't like being called Norma or Jean. It had to be together, both names as if it were all one: NormaJean. Anything else and it was she, herself, not her name, that was being abbreviated. It was as if a person with only one name was incomplete and unimportant. Not that Norma Jean had *done* anything in her life of any importance, that wasn't necessary. She was important because she was Norma Jean. Nothing else could possibly be added to that.

"God moves in mysterious ways, his wonders to perform," Norma Jean commented. "I guess we can praise the Lord for the accident, at least they died together."

Something inside Tim went hot. Why praise the Lord? God didn't have much to do with it, dammit. A drunk driver crossed the center line and hit them head-on. Yes, it was a good thing they were together. But why can't it just be life. It happens. Let it be a mystery. Getting God in the middle of it robs the soul of its grief. Why use God as a pain pill or a narcotic; just believe that they are with Jesus and we don't have to feel anything. We can even pretend to be happy about it. We can celebrate a life rather than grieve a death. But why do that? Why not feel it? Why not let the grief erode deep in the psyche? Wouldn't it make us more compassionate? Wouldn't it deepen our appreciation of life and our friends and our family? If we numb the pain, we numb life itself.

He wanted to scream his thoughts. He wanted to tell the whole room how shallow he thought they were, how shallow he thought religion was. He wanted to, but, of course, he didn't. He never did.

"I'm going to get a cup of coffee," Tim said as he pushed his chair away from the table. "Can I get you anything?"

"No, I'm OK." Karl responded. Norma Jean said nothing.

Tim paused, looking down at her. She glanced up at him and shook her head. Tim turned and walked toward the line of tables at the front of the social hall. At the far end were two large coffee urns with a stack of Styrofoam cups between them. The one on the left had a small sign hanging over the handle: DECAF. Tim put his cup under the other one and let the dark, steaming liquid rise nearly to the brim.

"You're one of Reverend Wilson's boys, aren't you?" The voice was a deep baritone with a little bit of Louie Armstrong's gravel in it. Tim didn't recognize it. He turned to face the speaker. When their eyes met, Tim felt a sudden rush in his head. He spilled his coffee. When he looked down, he noticed his hand was trembling slightly.

"Here," the baritone said as he held out a napkin. "I didn't mean to startle you. My name is Richard."

"Tim. Yes, I'm oldest." He answered as he took a sip of coffee. His voice was dry and it was hard to swallow.

Richard was a few inches taller than Tim with light sandy hair that was combed straight back. His eyes were an electric blue with a playful softness that was both mysterious and inviting. His day-old beard emphasized the strength of his jaw and gave him a dangerous or maybe an adventurous look.

"Too bad about the accident. Both your mom and dad. That's

tragic. I'm sorry for your loss," Richard remarked, and then added, "I understand the drunk driver had been arrested before and was driving on a suspended license."

"Yeah, that's what we were told. I guess he's still in the hospital." Tim paused, coughed, and cleared his throat. Hot tears formed behind his eyelids. Up to this moment Tim had not shown any emotion. He had kept his mind occupied with his internal arguments about all the religious stuff going on around him. But there was something about this man, about Richard, that allowed Tim to let the tension go and made him want to lean into his strong chest and sob. He wanted to be held and understood.

Tim had never been really honest with his parents, never shared the real stuff that was going on in his life. But they loved the Tim they thought they knew. They cared that he was OK and not too lonely living alone. They invited him over for dinner at least once a week. They reached out in whatever way they understood. It was Tim that held back, sharing only the external things: whether his art had been accepted in a particular show, if he won some recognition, what commissions he was working on. It was always about work or the house or some project, never how he felt, or who he cared for, or the things that made him happy or sad.

When he visited his parents, Tim encouraged them to reminisce and then would listen attentively to the familiar stories he had heard a hundred times. It was a bit boring but it was safer that way and Tim chose to play it safe. Now, he wasn't sure being safe was the best way to be. Maybe he had missed more than he gained. Either way, it was too late to change anything with his parents. He took a sip of coffee.

"It's a tragic loss for us, but I'm not sure either one of them could have survived very long without the other. Seventy years of living together and you can get kinda dependent on each other. It's still hard to believe they're gone, it's not real yet," Tim continued, trying to keep his voice steady. "I know I will go home tonight and expect a call in the morning asking if I'm OK and if I'll come over for dinner."

Five years ago, Tim had moved from across the state to be closer to them just in case he was needed for some special caregiving. They were both in good health at the time, but he knew when one of them died, things would get real difficult trying to take care of the other. Sometimes he had even tried to figure out which one would be the easiest to care for, which one he wanted to die first. It was a morbid thought. He never had figured it out. None of that mattered now.

"You live around here?" Richard asked.

Again, Tim felt the rush in his head. "'Bout five miles out of town," he managed after too long a silence. "Old farmhouse my uncle used to own when he was alive." Then added, "And you?"

"No. I'm down by Greenville," Richard answered.

Tim wasn't surprised. A lot of the family still lived in that area. Tim had been born there. But when Tim's dad entered the ministry, he had mostly served smaller churches in the northern part of the state. He took another sip of coffee. His hand was still a little shaky.

"I'd like to see the farmhouse sometime," Richard offered, his voice even more seductive.

"Now is not a good time." Tim knew what was happening. He'd been approached before. "Maybe some other time." Tim refilled his coffee and, as politely as possible, excused himself and headed back to Karl's table.

Back at the table, Tim stared at Karl and wondered if his attitude about homosexuality had changed. They had had that discussion years ago when Tim was secretly and desperately searching for some support, some way of believing that he was OK.

"Of course, it's a sin," Karl had answered without hesitation or seeming surprised by the question. "The Bible says it's an abomination unto man."

Yes, Tim had thought without saying it out loud. *The Bible also says that eating shrimp is an abomination, big deal.*

During the last few years in the church, Tim had found it more and more difficult to keep a lid on what had bubbled just beneath the surface since he was in middle school. He was trapped in an ongoing conflict of saying one thing Sunday morning and burning with an unquenchable passion to do exactly the opposite on Friday night; taking long drives to strange cities where he wouldn't be recognized; sitting in his parked car at some rest area to watch.

Back then he blamed Satan. It was a spiritual battle being fought out in his groin. He would sit in the dark of his car and sob his prayers, press his head hard against the steering wheel, begging God to heal him of this terrible disease; to forgive him for having gotten this far. Then, filled with shame and remorse, he would drive home and finish his sermon. He could remember times when one of his members, William, would come in for counseling. Sometimes as William talked, Tim would feel the heat of his penis pressing hard against his trousers. He would find it difficult to concentrate on what was being said. When William was leaving, Tim quickly focused his attention on the papers on his desk so he wouldn't have to stand up and reveal the bulging desire that had occupied his mind. Then, after he was in his office alone he would fall to his knees and beg God to forgive him. He would sometimes pray all night.

William was not an isolated case, there were other times and other men. Each time Tim was filled with remorse and shame. Maybe it was this terrible secret that had pointed out the problem with the creation story, the plants before the sun. Maybe this is what drove him to study the Bible relentlessly to find other errors. Maybe he had run out of words simply because the things he was supposed to say had all collided with his passion and gotten jumbled up somewhere below his belt.

What he knew then, and was even more certain of now, was that a great burden was lifted the day he left his resignation in the Board Room and walked to the art supply store. He no longer blamed the devil or anyone or anything. He was no longer ashamed of being Tim, whatever that meant.

It wasn't easy getting there, getting to the place of accepting himself, of being at peace inside his own skin. Once the restraint of the ministry and church and God was erased, all hell broke lose in his life. A monster had emerged from the basement of his soul, a monster that he had locked up tight and starved for years—and it was hungry. Its appetite seemed insatiable.

He didn't see his family very much during this time. He didn't want them to know or even try to guess or speculate about how he was living his life. He came home to visit only a couple of times over the seven or eight years immediately after his resignation from the church. He didn't want to try to explain the change in careers because he might give something away. He might evoke their disapproval. He still was not living his own life; he was being driven by passions he couldn't seem to control and a need for approval he knew he didn't deserve.

It wasn't until he was diagnosed with cancer that he finally came to terms with himself. Looking back, it was a wonder that he didn't have HIV/AIDS. Cancer was a blessing. At least there was hope for a cure. There was surgery and radiation and chemotherapy, there was a chance at survival. Lying in the hospital awaiting surgery, Tim had crashed headlong into his own mortality. During those hours alone, late at night, when the hospital hummed softly and nobody was coming to visit, Tim wept bitterly. He wept his rage that at one time he had believed that his God had both created him the way he was, and condemned him for being that way at the same time. He wept his anguish as he suffered his own internal condemnation. He was exhausted from trying desperately to be something different than what he was, and at the same time being driven by it. He cursed himself and his church for preaching that his condition, his homosexuality, could be healed, and for Tim, the lack of such a healing only drove his shame deeper.

When he awoke from the anesthesia and after visiting hours had ended and his family had left for the day, Tim found himself strangely at peace. Having no idea how successful his treatments would be, life became precious, and with that feeling, Tim became precious. Not in spite of his sexual orientation, but rather, because of it. For the first time in his life he let go of his self-condemnation, his self-hatred, and embraced who he was. He began to accept that it might be a blessing rather than a curse.

Again, he wept into the night, but this time it was a joyful weeping, tears of gratitude flowed silently. It was like discovering that someone he thought was dead, someone he loved very much, was not dead at all, but very much alive and well. A swamp of self-loathing had been drained and replaced by a flowing spring of sweet, fresh water. He drank deeply.

When he had left the hospital, he walked more confidently. The wild parties ended. His paintings took on new vitality and intensity. A few years after his surgery Tim had met Anthony at the Greater Michigan Art Show; they had fallen in love and began to share their lives together. It was a stable, committed relationship, but still Tim invited his folks over for dinner only when Anthony was out of town. He took great pains to make sure there was no evidence of someone else living at the farmhouse, so there would be no uncomfortable question. He had fully intended to come out to his family, to take that final step regardless of the consequences. But, in the end he had run out of time. He had procrastinated too long. Three days ago, he had lost forever the opportunity to be honest with his parents.

He sat for a long time staring into the dark sediment in his coffee cup. Then he looked up, first at Norma Jean, then Karl. "I'll meet you at the house around ten tomorrow morning and we can start sorting stuff out. Trash, Goodwill, keepers. But plan on coming over to the farmhouse for dinner?" A thin smile began to work its way across his lips. "We'll be tired of their stuff by then and it will give us a break. I'll throw something in the slow-cooker and it'll be ready whenever we are."

"Sounds good to me," Karl said.

"Sure, OK." Norma Jean added.

"Good, see ya in the morning. I'm outa here." He stood and, as he extended his hand, Karl pulled him awkwardly over the table and gave him a hug. He shook Norma Jean's hand and turned toward the door.

When he stepped outside, the storm had ended and the sky was beginning to clear. As he looked up, the ice on the tree branches made broken, concentric halos around the nearly full moon as it emerged from behind a ragged cloud. He was only part way down the sidewalk when he heard a familiar voice.

"Hey." It was Anthony.

"What are you doing here?" Tim asked, obviously glad to see him.

"Been waiting for you. Thought you might need a friend. I know how you are about your family."

The two men embraced for a long time. Then Tim looked up and Anthony gently kissed him on the lips.

"Thanks. I needed that," Tim whispered. Then he asked, "Where are you parked?"

"Next to you," Anthony answered. As they walked toward the cars, they had their arms around each other.

"Meet me at the market," Tim said, breaking the comfortable silence. "There's some things we need to pick up. We're having company for dinner tomorrow evening and I'd like it to be kinda special."

Again, a mischievous smile worked its way across Tim's lips.

About the author:

Terry Dickinson grew up in parsonages in several northern Michigan rural communities, earned a BS degree in math and physics, briefly taught high school math, and then worked most of his adult life as a visual artist before trying his hand at writing. His story of raising an orphaned fawn in the aftermath of his wife's death from cancer appeared in *Country Extra*. He has since remarried and at sixty-six he and his wife live near Traverse City, Michigan and are remodeling the old farmhouse once owned by his late aunt and uncle.

The story, "The Funeral Dinner", emerged from years of

observing the collision of values inherent in groups that profess to be loving and compassionate and at the same time isolate themselves into groups of "us" whose efforts for purity gives license to condemn "them". Further influencing the narrative are several friends who are gay and Terry has observed their struggles for self-acceptance, their defense against shame, and the subtle and often unintentional ways that good, well-meaning people reinforce that shame. Then add to that mix the hypocrisy of those whose sexual interest are at odds with their religious teachings and how that secret corrodes something important inside and leaves a person disconnected from the self. Funerals often force families together who might otherwise avoid each other, providing the perfect stage on which to explore the tension between keeping a secret or coming out.

AFTER THE DREAM: A MODERN FABLE
©2009 by Pauline A. Salvucci

The woods are my refuge, my calm. Hand-in-hand the little girl walked with me. We were silent. No need to talk. Just look, listen. All around us there was life. Trees breathed with the wind. Leaves rustled and twigs snapped beneath our feet. We played a game to see who could walk softly, making no sound. We both lost. I wondered how the Indians did it. I don't know. It's a skill, maybe an art, soundless walking. Creatures scampered out of our range of vision. They weren't soundless, either. Only the Indians were soundless, rendering homage to forest and woods.

I cocked my head and listened, then tugged at the child's hand. I heard distant noises through the woods, a rhythmic *thud, thud, thud*. I turned and strained to see. My pulse beat faster and I felt fear twist my stomach. And I am afraid of the unknown.

Again, I turned and looked. I saw it. A bear. Big. Brown. Ferocious-looking. Running towards us. My hands broke out in sweat and I pulled the child to face me. "Don't be afraid," I said to her. "I know how to keep us safe. Come." I began to run, pulling her after me. She turned to look back and I shouted, "No, just run. I know the way."

Crashing through the undergrowth, I headed toward the ocean, toward the rocks and the sound of surf, pulling—almost dragging—the child after me. We'd be safe there. I felt it. I knew it. We climbed, jumping from one rock to another, the child at my heels. My feet were steady, I never let go of her small hand. Mine sweated, but I held tight to hers.

When we reached the top of the rock, I pushed her behind me and told her to be still. My heart was beating frantically and my chest hurt, my breathing was quick and shallow. I was sweating from head to foot. The ocean breeze chilled me as I turned to face the bear.

"Stop," I demanded. "What do you want?"

The animal looked at me through his small, dark eyes. He opened his mouth, threw back his head, and roared. Saliva dripped from his wide jaws. I was terrified, but I roared back. He stood on his hind legs, towering, letting me know that he could kill me with one swat of his gigantic paw. I stood my ground and looked at him squarely and then, without thinking, I took a step closer. I motioned for the child not to follow.

"This is my territory," the bear growled. "Stay out of the woods. You don't belong here."

"The woods are in my soul. They are part of me. I need to come here," I said.

"Then you risk death." The bear growled, falling on all fours, and moved closer to me.

I did the unthinkable: I dropped down on all fours and the bear again roared his threat and moved closer. I caught his scent. "I am part of you and you are part of me," I said. "Teach me, and I will teach you."

"You have nothing to teach me," he growled.

"You have something to teach *me*," I responded, my fear sharp, unsure if he would attack. I knew he smelled my fear.

"I will kill you," he growled, shaking his massive head from side to side. Then he stared straight at me and added, "Easily, and the child too."

"Yes, you can kill us. But you can also teach me, and I can teach the child. Killing me is easy. Teaching me is harder."

The bear was curious, but wary. "Teach you what?"

"Teach me about your strength, your instincts."

"Why?" the bear wanted to know.

"Because I am part of you and you are part of me."

"What do you want to learn?"

"I want to learn about you, but I do not want to be killed."

The bear shook his massive bulk as if to shake away my words. I reached out my hand. "Teach me," I said. "I want to learn about what is different and the same between you and me."

The bear stared at me. I was barely breathing. All of my senses were tuned to his next move. And while I waited for him to respond, I knew my desire was genuine. This bear could teach me.

"You have much to learn," he said. "Everything is not always as it seems. You choose to be blind, but if you want me to teach you, then you must open your eyes and see how you are like me."

Defensively, I cried, "I'm not like you. I am not a killer."

"But you are," the bear growled. "Only you choose not to see it. You cannot learn from me unless you are willing to see that you, too, are a killer."

I wanted to cry, to run away. "I am not like you," I screamed and tears streamed down my face.

The child behind me, who had been standing still, moved closer and placed her tiny hand on my shoulder. "Yes, you are," she whispered. "You kill even though you say you don't."

I turned to look at her. I was stung by her words.

"How am I a killer?" I whispered to her.

Her eyes were solemn and I felt her look straight through me. "When you are afraid," she said, "you kill. You kill what frightens you."

I was on all fours looking up at her. I couldn't speak, could scarcely breathe.

The bear rumbled deep in his throat. "The child speaks the truth. This is what you must acknowledge. Then I will teach you about my strength and the wildness of the woods, but not until then. When you learn about instinct and the life of wildness, you will belong to the woods. You will walk the earth a free woman. 'Til then you are living half a life. The choice is yours."

The bear stood on his hind legs again and roared. It was deafening. Then he dropped his front paws to the ground and walked away.

"Wait," I called. "Where are you going?"

"Come and find me when you are ready to learn," he growled and disappeared into the thickness of the woods.

I stood silently and watched the bear as he lumbered into the forest. I felt lost and alone for a moment in spite of the fact that he had frightened me.

When I turned to look for the child, she, too, was gone. I peered this way and that, calling her. Silence. Where had she gone? It was as if she vanished like a wispy cloud. Not a sign of her was left in my forest world.

Feeling exhausted, I found a patch of moss next to a large oak tree and lay down. The sky was azure and the leaves whispered softly in the breeze while birds twittered one to another.

I fell into a deep sleep and dreamed I was in a dark cave within the boundary of a cemetery. The walls of the cave were hewn of chiseled rock, the floor was hard dirt. The only light was by candles scatted among varying levels on the rock walls. I smelled the dank air around me and watched as a woman appeared before my eyes. She was tall and ethereal looking, and with her were two other women, smaller in stature and rounder in body. Around her, she wore a dark cloak. Her hair, too, was dark and long and I could see her features: high cheek bones, an aquiline nose, and deep, penetrating eyes.

It was then that I noticed several small plants which she held in her left hand. When I looked at them, she explained she was about to plant them to appease the dark spirits. I held my breath. She looked at me and offered some plants. I reached to take them. I was mesmerized by her presence. She both attracted and repulsed me. I sensed a danger in her that was mysterious, yet appealing.

When I took the plants, two little people appeared at my side. Where they had come from, I didn't know. I neither feared them, nor was I particularly drawn to them. They stayed close to me as I fastened eyes with the woman. Witch Woman. She was alluring in her presence which drew me and frightened me simultaneously. In spite of this, or because of it, I allowed myself to open to her until I felt a burning intensity and then drew away in confusion and fear.

"I won't help you plant flowers to your dark spirits," I told her. She stood silent, her eyes not wavering from mine. I tore my eyes away from her and, standing, I threw the flowers to the dirt floor and turned to flee the cave, calling to the two little people to follow me. I shouted, telling them I would protect them. "Just follow me," I gasped as I ran this way and that into the darkened cemetery, looking for the way out.

I have no idea how long I ran with the little people in tow. I only hoped it was far enough away from Witch Woman, her cave, and the graveyard. I entered a small town and looked frantically to find refuge, for I feared that Witch Woman would kill me should she find and catch me.

Across the road, I saw a large picture window with a number of religious icons on glass shelves. They beckoned me. I walked to the door, opened it quickly, and entered, leaning my back against the hard-polished wood, slamming the door shut. My eyes took in row after row of glass and ceramic crosses and statues of saints. A strong odor of incense assaulted my nose and I coughed. Looking out the window, I searched the road for Witch Woman and her minion but saw nothing of them.

I closed my eyes for a moment and sighed. Perhaps I would be safe here. When I opened my eyes and peered between the shelves, I saw no one attending the store and, although I cried out for help, no one came. In my fury and fear, I turned and, with outstretched arm, began knocking to the floor and smashing as many crosses and statues as I could. Once I began breaking the glass and ceramic icons, I couldn't stop. It was as if I was possessed, so furious was my rage.

Spent, I looked around at the damage. The two little people stared at me, never once participating in my rampage. Then they clapped their tiny hands and high-pitched laughter rang from their throats. I felt proud and powerful and, without another thought of Witch Woman or her helpers, I the opened the wooden door we had entered and walked out into the fresh air and gleaming sun.

No sooner had I taken two steps, I felt two strong arms tighten around me, and my face and body were cradled deep within the soft folds of a dark cape. While surprised and frightened, I struggled briefly but soon I felt my body relax and slumber came swiftly.

When I awoke, I found myself again in Witch Woman's cave. A moment of panic caused me to rise quickly to my feet, but I couldn't move. I looked down to find garlands of flowers and vines woven around my ankles, making movement impossible.

Witch Woman stood before me and then pointed her finger at me. "Sit," she said.

I stood defiantly until her minions and the two little people took me firmly by the shoulders and arms and pushed me into a stone chair behind me. "What do you want"? I demanded.

"It's not what *I* want, the question is what *you* want," she replied.

I stared back at her in silence.

"I am told that you wish to learn about the bear's strength and the forest which you say is alive in your soul."

My eyes narrowed and I felt my heart increase its beating. "Who told you that"? I snarled.

Witch Woman slowly circled the stone chair in which I sat and came once again to stand before me. "You wish to learn and yet you run. First from the bear and then from me. What do you expect to learn when you run from that which lies within you? Did the bear not tell you he would teach you when you were ready to learn?"

I looked at the Witch and responded slowly. "I told the bear and I will tell you, I am not a killer, like the both of you."

"You asked the bear to teach you about the forest, about his strength, his nature, his instincts, and you came of your own will to my cave. You cannot learn from the deep instinctual nature of the bear, nor can you learn from my dark wisdom. You can not take from others when you refuse to enter your own forest."

Her words stung me. I was afraid she had spoken the truth. I had feared the bear yet challenged him to teach me, while I denied the truth he knew about me. I had refused to acknowledge that the dark power of his nature was also in my own. I feared the power of the bear and Witch Woman, each to live both under the sun and within the darkness.

Looking up into Witch Woman's face, tears flowed from my eyes. I realized I was a sham and a coward. I wanted to live only in the sun. To that end, I persevered in seeing myself in only the best of lights, helping others and showing kindness. And yet in my blindness, I judged and feared those whose spirits were freer than my own. I refused to accept that as the day ends in shadow and dark night, so, too, must I be willing to embrace the shadow and dark night within myself.

And then I remembered that before Witch Woman returned me to her cave, I had run and found a shop which I thought would offer me comfort and protection. And instead it was empty except for cold glass and ceramic crosses and statues of saints. I recalled the wicked pleasure I felt in smashing as many icons as I could break. And it was only after I had created all the rubble that I felt no fear and was able to walk away from the store and breathe fresh air.

I was stunned. I looked at the witch and for the first time she smiled at me. It was as if she could read my mind. "Yes" she said. "You took your first step."

"It felt wonderful!" I cried. "I felt free from the old dead fear, but I didn't know it then. I only understand that now. What do I do now to learn what lies within"?

"Decide if you are truly ready to make this journey," Witch Woman responded. "I will show you the door but you must make the decision to enter. And if you do, no matter what you find, the discoveries are yours to make, no matter what they are."

I took a deep breath and nodded my assent.

"Then close your eyes and wait," she said. "When you are ready, open them and always remember that this is your journey, your choice, and you must decide how you will travel through its darkness."

Again, I nodded and then closed my eyes and waited. I heard nothing. I continued to wait. Nothing. Becoming somewhat impatient, I opened one eye and looked around. Witch Woman was gone, as were her minions and the two little people. I opened my other eye. I was alone in the cave. The candles still burned, casting flickering light around the dark walls. The dank air had turned warmer and as I looked down at my ankles, which had been bound by garlands of flowers and vines, I began to see movement. Replacing the garlands and vines were all forms of snakes, small and large, twisting and slithering. I felt them around my ankles and moving between my toes. Their bodies were dry. Some were smooth while others were rough.

I gasped and opened my mouth to scream but no sound came. My heart raced as if it would burst from my chest and my mouth felt as dry as desert sand.

Breathe, I commanded myself. After all, I said, I was ready to undertake this journey, but my God, *snakes?*

In spite of my brave willingness when the Witch was present, I now felt terrible fear and horror. I looked again and saw the snakes began to weave and wind their way up my calves and behind my knees. The sensation was unbearable.

Breathe, I told myself. *BREATHE!* I took one breath after another, gulping and trying to deepen each and every inhalation while exhaling in shaky spurts. *Slowly, slowly,* I told myself as the serpents wove their lithe bodies around my waist and breasts and then my neck. When they reached my face, the panic returned full blast. I closed my mouth tight, pressing my lips together and clenched my jaw until it ached. Although I wanted to close my nostrils, too, I knew I couldn't and so I squeezed my eyes shut as I felt a serpent slither close to my left ear.

"Remember," the snake hissed.

"Remember what?" I croaked, my voice a whisper. The snakes stopped moving. I felt their bodies reposition, encircling my own from head to toe, and then it was as if a great wind fell upon me and in unison they hissed, *"Remember."*

At that moment, my body went limp within the snakes' embrace and I felt the sweet sensation of floating. I breathed deeply and the memories began to surface. One by one they came. Words from the past. Harsh words from painful times.

If you leave, you will find yourself in the muck and mire of life.

You think you're smarter than me? You're not. You're nothing and you'll never be anything, so accept it and shut up.

*You know what's wrong with you? You're...*and the litany of my faults, real and imagined, poured forth like poison.

The memories came fast and furious, and the words spoken to me long ago became more cruel, vile, and hateful. I remembered faces contorted in contempt, spitting out words and feelings that struck as quick as lightening. I remembered feeling shocked to my core. I felt as if my body had dissolved and melted into the ground where I stood. I couldn't speak. It was as if I were struck dumb.

I clamped my eyes tight and felt my throat constrict. How long had it been since these words were spoken? Years ago, but as the memories surfaced it was if they were happening in the moment. Heinous words, spoken in anger and in the attempt to inflict pain, humiliation, and fear. Why is it that the people who are supposed to love us say such terrible things?

Tears trickle from the corners of my eyes and spill down my cheeks onto the snakes covering my face. And as I struggled to control my tears the snakes spoke to me again in unison.

"Do not fight your tears. Let them flow. Be brave. You must remember. We are here to hold you."

I was stunned at their words and yet found a strange comfort in them. Had not Witch Woman told me that I must choose to follow where this journey led me? Had I not told her that I would?

The snakes moved again, as if to encourage me to stay with my memories. I felt their embrace give me strength. And with that the dam broke, and I began to sob. My body shook and my soul trembled as I felt the pain of those memories hit me full in my soul. I felt as if my heart were breaking and that if I weren't held by the snakes, I would dissolve within the flood of tears I could not stop.

I don't remember how long I cried, but it must have been a long time. I was wrung out, exhausted. I opened my eyes and took a deep, shuddering breath. It took a while before I could breathe normally again.

"Sleep now," the snakes whispered. "When you wake, we will be here."

And with that promise I fell asleep.

When I woke, I stretched lazily and the snakes repositioned themselves around my body. How strange to be comforted by such primal creatures. How could this be? I wondered again.

"I wish to stand and move," I said, and with that the snakes began their slow, easy unwind from my body and once again curled themselves around my feet and ankles. I reached down and gently touched them, one by one. Their black tongues flicking, they swayed facing me. As I stood, they crawled a small distance away, watching my face. I stretched my body, my arms high over my head, my muscles relaxed. I began to dance slowly, winding my body around the walls of the cave, moving my arms and legs and hips to some interior music. My body felt free and almost weightless.

When I looked at the snakes, they were slithering back into the deep crevices of the cave walls.

"Wait," I cried. "Where are you going?"

"We have done what we came to do, you must travel the rest of your journey alone now," they said.

"I will miss you. Thank you."

Without another word they disappeared.

How strange, I thought. Snakes were the last thing I ever thought I would feel comforted by. What was it about those primitive creatures that caused me to recall such painful memories and release them through tears? And had I really released my feelings or were they still lodged within my heart, ready to burst forth unbidden and overwhelm me again? What do I do with all this? I wasn't sure but I knew my journey would continue.

I sighed and gathered myself and walked out into the sunshine of the cemetery, strolling along the paths, looking at the headstones and wondering about the people buried beneath them. I wondered what kind of lives they led and if they had been meaningful. I wondered if they had been happy and what was important to them. I wondered how they died and who missed them. I wondered who loved them and whom they had loved.

Looking around to see how far I had wandered from the cave, I noticed the end of one path open to the forest. I hesitated. I didn't know if I was ready to meet the bear should he find me, but I was hungry and so I moved into the forest to look for berries and nuts.

Sitting on a large rock in the sun and eating the sweet fruit and nuts I had foraged, my mind wandered back to the incidents in the cave. The snakes had taught me something about myself. Their embrace and injunction to *"remember"* had somehow allowed me to recall memories long forgotten. The thing that surprised me was how easily the memories came and how real they were. My memories were as primitive as the snakes themselves. They rose from deep within me and I wondered if what I had asked the bear and Witch Woman to teach me had something to do with them. I remembered part of my conversation with the bear.

"I'm not like you. I am not a killer."

"But you are, only you choose not to see it. You can not learn from me unless you are willing to see that you, too, are a killer."

I lay back on the rock, let my mind wander, and welcomed the warm sun on my body. The more I thought, the more confused I became. Frustrated, I sat up and began the slow walk home. Suddenly very tired, I wanted to go home and get some much-needed sleep.

That night I slept and dreamed.

I was standing in a circle with the faces of those who had hurt me in life jeering at me and poking at my body with their fingers. I turned slowly within the circle and felt impotent to stop them.

Blood trickled from the corners of my eyes and I screamed. Their faces contorted, ugly, accusing, and their hate-filled words rose in frenzied screams.

Several huge rats crept up my pant leg and settled there and on my left hip, their yellow teeth clicking in anticipation, eyes staring fiercely at the faces surrounding us. Rain hammered on a bedroom window and turned to clots of blood.

"Get them!" I screamed. The rats jumped amidst the jeering faces circling us and began tearing them to pieces. The room was full of blood. It smelled like copper. I stood and looked around me at shredded skin ripped in chunks lying on the floor, plastered to the furniture and splattered on the walls. Disembodied eyes stared back at me. I smiled.

Three hawks flew through the stained window into my room and began feasting on the dead and bloody flesh of my enemies.

"Yes! Yes! Yes!" I screamed, sitting up in bed, clutching my hammering chest, my body trembling, soaked in sweat and fear.

I sat in bed, running my hands over my face and gasping for breath, I thought, *My God, am I going nuts?*

Slowly I calmed myself and slid out of bed. I was a bit unsteady on my feet as I walked into the shower and turned on the water. Leaning against the back wall I felt the hot water hit and run over my body, washing away my sweat and calming me from the terrible excitement of my dream.

I dressed, took my journal from my desk and went to the kitchen to make coffee. As the coffee brewed, I closed my eyes and inhaled its strong scent of comfort filling the kitchen. When it was ready, I poured a large mug and sat for a while, pen in hand, sipping my coffee. I wrote five words in the middle of the next page in my journal:

Anger
Fury
Rage
Depression
Retribution

I looked at the words for a long time. The coffee in my cup grew cold. Somehow, I felt relaxed and comfortable. But I also felt something else. Anticipation. There is something else. There is much more.

I have met the bear and he has promised to teach me when I am ready. Witch Woman has offered me the door to open and the choice to make the journey. The snakes have given me great comfort in my terror. My dream has shown me the depth of my rage and pain and longing.

I pick up my pen and write:

I am ready. I can change.

About the author:

Pauline A. Salvucci was born in Massachusetts and resides in Westbrook, Maine with her rescue cat, Jack Kerouac. Her first career as a high school English literature and composition teacher was followed by a 25-year career as a licensed psychotherapist in private practice. She enjoys painting, jazz piano and reading. "After the Dream: A Modern Fable" is Pauline's first short story. She is currently working on its sequel. Pauline is also a jewelry designer and maker. Her jewelry is sold in retail stores in Maine.

AND WHY IS THAT AGAIN?
©2009 by Jean Tschohl Quinn

"Voya, get off the counter, you nosy thing." I push our Siamese down. The cat gives a half-hearted hiss to which I respond, "You old cranky hag." Just to prove that she still has some zip, she dashes silently out of the room. I re-adjust the phone to my ear. "Sorry, Jan. Anyway, how are they doing?"

"Well," Jan hesitates. She hates to say anything that might disappoint anyone. "Actually, they're having a great time. I'm sorry. They haven't even asked how you're doing."

"Don't apologize. What could be better than being with their cousins? You've been a lifesaver. Thanks for having them over. I'll be able to handle them by tomorrow after the follow-up exam." I swallow the big pink pill and then vaguely recall having taken one only an hour before. Oops.

"How are you feeling? I mean, really," she speaks in a conspiratorial whisper.

"I've got a fair amount of movement back. I've been icing my back and neck for two days now. Now I can't even get warm anymore."

"Where're Harris and Annie?"

"Out in the garage, I think. He's p-puttering." A giggle escapes me. "Ooh, the Vicodin is kicking in. I'm flying already. I think I took it too early. Geez, I am such a light weight." I lean against the counter to steady myself.

"And Annie? What's Annie up to?"

"She's barricaded up in her room again. What does she do up there? I think I'd rather not know. Ah, teenagers."

"Well, the boys are fine. Get some rest. And don't drink any alcohol, little sis," she adds in a sing-song.

"Well, I'm fine too. I'm not sleepy," I mock, "And I just might, big sis."

"Argh. Good night," she hangs up before I elaborate on my defiance. She worries that I might do things just because she tells me not to. She is right to worry.

I hang up the phone and rub my arms as vigorously as my medicated reflexes allow. I spy Harris' wine glass, half full, on the kitchen counter and down it in one swallow, pick up a large towel hanging over the back of a kitchen chair and go outside.

The night is clear and briskly cool. The moon is full but currently hiding behind the trees as I slide into our new Sundance 7000 Home Spa. Slowly, I reach for the control panel button: jets on *high*, lights on *whatever*.

The steam encircles me. The water's heat penetrates my body as the cold night air blows across my cheeks in an effort to call me back to reality. Looking up, I can see that the sky was still clear even as I watch the fog roll in from the coast. It is weird. That's all there is to it. Maybe, it is the bubbles or the funny LED light show option we purchased. Sooo pretty.

The moon slowly climbs among the limbs of the surrounding trees, shifting the shadows around me. I'd be spooked if I weren't just so, so relaxed.

Up from the moonlit gully, a dark figure emerges. I gasp. He approaches, dressed in black. Without a word, he discards his cape. His *cape*? I must be hallucinating, so I palm my eyes for a moment to clear them. He strips and slides into the hot spa across from me.

There he sits, pale in the pool of blood-red water of the Sundance 7000's light show.

"Who are you?"

"Goood eeevening," he says with a thick Hungarian accent, "I am your friendly neighborhood vampire." It's more like *wampire*, than *vampire*.

Why am I imagining a wampire—I mean, vampire? "What you are doing here?"

"I'm suuuuure you can guess." He smiles.

Well, I do like why-do-vampires-just-drink-blood jokes.

Because root beer makes them burp.

I giggle to myself.

"I'd like to bite your neck."

"Oh, pulleez," is the clever retort I muster.

"All right then, why do you think I'm here?" The accent falls away like pine needles from a six-week-old Christmas tree. He sounds like someone out of *Fargo*, like all my cousins back east, like a sitcom character writ large.

Because milk would make them moo.

"You, apparently, are my painkiller, wine, and heat-induced hallucination this evening. So, tell me your story."

"You know my story."

I cross my arms in sloppy defiance. "I know the Bram Stoker version. It's lame. The rest of them are lost on me. Why are you here?"

He copies my crossed arms with a campy pout. "Look. This is *your* hot-tub therapy, not mine."

"Okay. First of all, the *Fargo* accent isn't working. What other speech patterns do you have?"

"Ghetto?" His skin darkens.

"Too Wesley Snipes. Too *Blacula*."

"Bostonian?" His skin returns to pale.

I shake my head immediately, aghast at the implications. "My husband is from Massachusetts. What would my friends think when I tell them about this?"

"You're planning to tell them?"

A rabbit scurries across the yard. I resist the impulse to consider Bunnicula.

"Upper crust Brit?" He turns even paler.

"Hmmm." I consider it. I've always had a soft spot for the Queen's pasty-faced subjects. "What? Ho? Might I ask your permission to suck out a bit of your blood? Won't take but a tick. Pardon me." It is my best Jeeves-and-Wooster. Prudently, I drop the imitation, "Naw, I don't think so."

"Manchester? Welsh? Scottish brogue?" With each offering he looks vaguely like some popular British actor or another. He stops on Sean Connery (Darby-O'Gill-and-the-Little-People Sean Connery, not Indiana-Jones-and-the-Last-Crusade Sean Connery.)

I shrug. "Can't tell the difference, quite frankly. Naw. Where hasn't a vampire been from before?"

"You can have me," he pauses to great effect, "be from wherever you like."

I roll my eyes and rub them again, "Be gone, imaginary vampire." I peek through my fingers. He smiles, giving me a playful little wave.

I slap the surface of the water, "Dang. I thought that would work."

"Dang? That's all the cursing you can manage?"

"I don't curse. Maybe the world does, but I don't." This is a nice fantasy, in the heat and fog and moonlight. "Hmmm."

We watch the churning waters a while. "How about a luscious Portuguese accent with charmingly imperfect English?" I stop to ponder, "Oh, from Goa actually—Portuguese and Indian mix."

A well-groomed mustache appears above his lip. His nose is now more pronounced. Thick, tresses of black curls hang to his shoulders. His eyes are almost black. His skin darkens to something smooth, rich, and bittersweet.

Because cocoa burns their lips.

We sit in an odd silence, not completely comfortable but not unpleasantly so. I puzzle over him. He stares at me, doing that vampire thing. His seduction is draining me of my will to stay lucid. Perhaps just a fanciful, private romp for my own pleasure would be all right under the circumstances...

The air jets stop. The timer is funky on the Sundance 7000. The great burbling gives way to increasingly tinier bubbles that dance and tickle.

Because champagne costs too much.

The lights shift to a pink/red cycle, maybe it's a chromatherapy "sexy" setting or something. If I had ever bothered to read the manual, I'd know.

The water clears, displaying everything about my bath mate. I mean *everything*: The broad chest, the tattoo of an elaborate valentine over his heart that reads "Do not pierce" in an even more elaborate script, well-muscled limbs, strong elegant hands, and quite the endowment. I try to concentrate on the tattoo, thinking that it would be better in Portuguese: *Não Perfure.* Maybe it was *Nenhuma Entrada* (No Entrance) or *Não Entre* (Do Not Enter) or *Há uma primeira vez para tudo* (There's a first time for everything).

Such ponderings are not completely effective at distracting me from all there was to see. I look deeper into the water and then turn away out of a repressed, guilt-laden habit that has been with me since puberty.

He looks at me disappointedly and waves his hands to create a Speedo or something like one. No, really, it looks okay...better than okay.

"Hmmm. What shall I do with you?" I murmur.

He moves towards me, "Let me show you what I can do." My hands shoot up in protest; he settles back. "But I have so many powers. Look, there is no reflection of me."

The water is quite still. And yes, there is no reflection. He looks rather pleased with himself. I begrudgingly say, "Impressi... Wait a minute. Nothing would reflect; it's lit from below."

He shrugs impishly.

I scoff. "Look, every person I know eventually can no longer see her-or-himself in a mirror. Eventually, we're all replaced by some old stranger that stares back at us. Big deal."

"But I can slip in and out so quietly. I am virtually unseen." He leans into me.

"Whoop-de-doo. Every woman over fifty gets the power of invisibility in this society. As soon as she's no longer considered desirable by some increasingly narrow standard of desirability, *poof!* She's gone. I can walk through a mall and not be noticed at all. Dozens of young people—especially young men, I might add—don't see me. I'm not even part of their consciousness. Oh, they'll take advice from each other on subjects they know nothing about and believe them, all the while dismissing the very people who *do* know." I glance up at the window of Annie's room and pull my harangue back into check, almost. "They don't know what they're missing."

The vampire laughs freely, generously. "No, they don't." He slides around the molded spa seat to inveigle his arm around me. "I would *never* ignore you."

It is my turn to laugh, "And it would cost me dearly. It would cost hours of energy to keep it that way. That's what a vampire does." I pinch his cheek for good measure. "He sucks up energy."

Pouting, he pulls his arm back from me. His shoulders slump. His eyes plead like those of a sweet puppy. This time, I put my arm around him. "Oh, baby, don't pout. It's just what you do, I mean, symbolically speaking. You're creepy—"

Interrupted with his mournful sigh, I take his chin in my free hand and look directly into his eyes. "Aaaaand alluring, because that's what people who suck the life out of people are. You're just a psychological archetype, honey-lamb."

He whimpers again, and I squeeze him tighter with disturbingly maternal instincts.

"Aaaargh!" I growl in indignation as his hand shifts to fondle me. I stand up in the center of the tub, arms akimbo. "See? You just keep taking. You even took my sympathy."

"I'm sorry," he moans piteously as he pulls his face into my stomach in artful regret. He hugs me desperately.

His heat wraps around me and I indulge in it. I grin, tousle his dark hair, and look up at the stars. We are mutually benefiting from each other, I can tell. Then I feel it—a sharp prick, no, two sharp pricks into my abdomen. I push him away. "You rat!"

He tosses his hands up. "Nothing ventured, nothing gained!" Casually draping his arms along the back of the tub, he settles back in his place and flashes a boyish, fanged grin.

"Nothing ventured, nothing gained, my ass."

He winks disarmingly.

"Maybe, just maybe, I'll let you have some fun. Maybe, maybe not." I am suddenly aware of the cold air around me. "Look, I'm not in much of a position to handle this. How about if you go?"

"But you said I'm just a hallucination. What harm can I do?"

I grin, "Well, with what's racing through my bloodstream right now, you'd probably get sick anyway."

He is making no attempt to leave, and I can see that he is scheming. He leans forward and takes my hands earnestly. "Well, I could just sit here and tell you a little story," he says, "just to entertain you. There could be a middle-aged woman..."

I glare at him. He plows on enthusiastically, clearly making it up as he goes along, "A bee-yoo-tiful, middle-aged woman—who meets a handsome young vampire."

I roll my eyes, "Same old, same old. Where's the meaning in that?"

That comment irritates him, "No, no, no. She's stalking him. At first, she starts out asking him for help with a few chores. Then she schedules his time. She starts mothering him. She nags him. She's so needy that she sucks the life out of him until he's too weak to do what he must. Pretty twisted, eh?"

"Screw you," I plop back into the water.

He smiles and leans back. "You wish."

Then I laugh. "Not bad, actually."

I'm sure that he'll just go away if I just quit thinking about him. As I reach for the light button to cycle it to another of the lighting programs, panic flits across his face, but he stays put. He practically coos and his accent is back thickly, "But you will be remembering me? You won't forget me, will you? You can't leave me now, because you are now mine."

"Maybe," I smirk at him. "Maybe not."

Because iced tea is too cold.

The program lights shift through shades of blues—silvery to near darkness. I lift my chin to gaze at the stars. Maybe shades-of-blue is the relaxation setting.

Voya jumps up from out of the darkness and steam. With nearly closed eyes, I watch her walk along the edge. She stops at his ear and hisses protectively. The vampire sighs, rolls his smoldering eyes, and flexes some muscles.

I say to Voya, "Never mind him. He's not really here."

Because pop tickles their noses.

The vampire lets his head loll back to gaze at the stars in mock boredom, but he is still quite aware of the cat's proximity. He suddenly hisses at her. Voya jumps down and disappears into the garden.

His eyes lock on the desk lamp shining from Annie's bedroom window.

I laugh nervously and splash him. "I think that'll be enough for now."

There is a small bang not too far off. The two of us look toward the house. The back door is swinging closed. It is Harris sauntering towards us.

Oh-so-swiftly, the vampire slips out of the tub and melts into the darkness.

Harris gives me a peck on the cheek, turns off the tub lights. Off go his t-shirt and track shorts. He poses and postures in the light of the moon now high in the sky. I dare not show that I find the striptease more comedic than enticing. Mind you, it's not bad. The vampire emerges from the shadows to do the same. There is no comparison. He moves with a virile grace that Harris can only imagine in his most adolescent mind. I do not object to either show.

A sudden gust of wind ends Harris' show and he leaps into the hot water.

Harris pushes one of my bathing suit straps off my shoulder, then the other as he kisses my neck. "Do you always wear a suit in your after dark tubby tubby times?"

His endearing goofiness seems corny in front of the "witness." Still, I play along, trying not to look at the derisive leer coming from the vampire now perched on the edge of the tub, his feet in the water, knees wide apart in an effort to tease. It is working.

I rivet my eyes on Harris' eyes and coo, "No, not always, but the light was still on in Annie's room when I came out. I wouldn't want to scare her into thinking her mom would go in the hot tub *nekked*. She'd probably freak."

"Well, there's no light on now. We're safe. She said goodnight to me twenty minutes ago."

We kiss. Harris tries to pull down the top of my suit.

"It's a two-piece," I mumble into his shoulder. I stifle a laugh as the vampire puts on cross-eyes and a goofy smile. The fangs remain.

"Huh?" the silver-tongued Harris asks.

"It's called a tankini. One up. One down."

He screws up his face while analyzing what I just said. He smiles and lifts the top, "Oh. I see how it works now."

The vampire moves in closer. Is he pouting? He, too, leans in and whispers, "I'll be right here as long as you want me."

I mouth the words, "Go away." I close my eyes and concentrate on Harris, but I can still feel the vampire's hot breath on my neck, tickling my ear. I push all my attention toward Harris.

He pulls away slightly and asks, "What's wrong?"

"Nothing! Just full of pain-killers," I say, hopefully in a genuine tone, and reel him back in.

"Feelin' no pain," Harris jokes in what I suspect is his idea of a sexy voice.

The vampire rises slowly and glides over the edge and out of the tub. He conjures a large, black towel and rubs himself provocatively with it. Entranced, I struggle to stay mindful of Harris and the in-the-tub activities.

The vampire wraps himself in his cape once more. He blows me a kiss and walks—no glides—into the house. He phosphoresces, which allows me to follow his movement through the kitchen, up the stairs, down the hall. The glow now pulsates in my daughter's bedroom. What...the...hell?

Why do vampires just drink blood? Because it comes in cute-looking, sweet-smelling, highly disposable, biodegradable containers.

About the author:

Jean Tschohl Quinn started out as a Wisconsinite, played at being a Virginian after college, pretended to be an Illinoisan for a while, is begrudgingly becoming a Californian but prefers to be considered a world citizen. A mathematician by degree, a musician by choice, a mom by—well, we all know the usual way one gets to be a mom—Jean started writing fiction a short time ago somewhat unexpectedly. She lives with her husband, three daughters and two dogs in some redwoods along the Central Coast of California.

REGRET
©2009 by Bernard Hofler

I woke before the sun was up and went out to the lake. It was mid-spring and still cool enough in the mornings for the mosquitoes not to be of bother first thing. As I wandered through the thinning of the trees that bordered the side of the lake, I saw her there. She was alone...

There are moments in time too surreal to be written down or spoken of. This was one of those moments...her presence made it so. She was sitting by the water's edge with a dog at her side, watching the sun rise. The sunlight was already beginning to glitter off the body of water before her. The animal's tail beat the ground with each stroke of her fingers across its head.

I wished only to see her face. Carefully I stepped out of the tree line, but a dry limb made the dog turn round and look for me. The light yelp of the animal made her turn from the orange and red sunlight just as it broke, lighting up the side of her face.

The world went silent as her eyes met mine. I couldn't speak for lack of words to say...

Seeing I was only a man and nothing to worry over, she turned back to the dawn of the new day. I was still standing at a distance when she rose and walked away.

For a solid month of mornings after, I went back to that same patch of trees hoping to get another glimpse of her by the water's edge. I regret standing there in awe and not walking over to speak with her. I regret not hearing her voice, not finding out her name.

Looking back now, it seems more of a dream, really. Was either of us really there? Did that sun really rise as brightly as I remember? Did it glisten off her face as I recall?

I'm an old man now and rarely return to the lake, but whenever I do, I think of that Angel in the distance and wish I had walked over and asked her name. It is one of my truest regrets, just as her face lit by the orange light is one of my strongest memories.

In the end our memories are what make us who we are...

About the author:

Bernard is a resident of northeastern North Carolina. "Regret" was written for a young woman by the name of Lisa Maguire and is the first of his short stories to be published.

SENIOR DISCOUNT
©2009 by LeeAnn Dickson

SHE:

"Damn young whippersnappers" she says, shuffling toward the checkout counter, using her cane to clear everyone out of her way.

A glow of pink scalp emanates through a few wisps of translucent hair on her head that is recklessly attached to a bowed back. Over her triple chins, adorned with wiry whiskers, a slash of ruby red lipstick is streaked on her frowning gash of a mouth. The faded Hawaiian muumuu hangs off her shoulders revealing the tips of her breasts which are resting on top of a swollen stomach. Purple veined calves peek between the tattered hem and the rims of her dingy tube socks. Her feet grow into ancient, dusty, black, sensible flat-soled shoes.

Through a Popeye squint and black bat-winged glasses balanced on the tip of her flushed veined nose, she takes her time to scan the sales receipt for errors and to make sure all discounts have been applied. Not caring the least little bit that the line of shoppers is now ten deep and growing. She stands slumped over and thinks *I'm too old to care enough to be polite.* She's a senior citizen and demands all the discounts and knows she is entitled to every dime off the final tally.

Looking around, she opens her wallet and slowly extracts cash and mines a single penny from the bowels of her cavernous, dilapidated pocket book. This takes time...since she sets all the bills and coins on the counter and has the cashier count them again.

After the transaction is complete, she crooks her head and looks over her shoulder and sizes up the cashier once more, grips her purse and purchases, and leaves the counter. Using her cane as a third leg, she hobbles out the door toward her old Buick.

ME:

I have no illusions of looking younger than my fifty-three years. Neither embarrassed by the aging process, nor planning to artificially appear younger. Choosing not to succumb to costly and painful surgery to emulate movie stars with muscles pulled up so tight it is a wonder they can touch the ground.

My vanities allow me a regular cut and color, potent day and nighttime moisturizers, lots of sunscreen, and workouts at the gym.

I was feeling particularly feisty one morning and decided to run some errands. I started the day by attending a forty-five minute X-Bike (stationary bike on steroids) workout. The lithe young teacher climbed aboard her bike on the stage in front of a crescent sea of cycles. The riders in their twenties took the front rows and the few over-thirties rode in the back with me.

The teacher's pierced belly-button ring shined like a tiny beacon on her flat belly, and her perky breasts squeezed out of the top of her day-glow-orange spandex sports bra. She started "her music" and screamed at us to stand-sit-gear-up-gear-down through headache inducing sounds.

Maybe the supple young nymphs in the room call that music; I think it is just a beat-driven din that blares out of human-sized speakers to keep your exhausted legs moving. Although my thighs sizzled, my legs kept going round and round to the pulsating pounding. My lungs heaved for every gasp of air.

Through nearly bursting eardrums, I detected familiarity in the noise. It was my cry-myself-to-sleep song when I was sixteen: Nilsson's "Without You." I had the 45 RPM single and used to listen to it every night, tears streaming into my pillow. I couldn't figure out why the guy I loved didn't love me. My dad finally let me down easy by simply saying, "I don't think he likes girls."

I sweated on the bolted down bike and heard the words masked by heavy drums. *Blam Blam*. The lively beat went against the solemn lyrics and my gloomy memories. Kids! Can't they write their own songs?

After I got home, I drank my daily strawberry-blueberry-antioxidant smoothie and read the newspaper. Showered, slipped on my denim not-too-short shorts, a turquoise V-neck Tee, flip flops and hoop earrings. After a touch of mascara and lip gloss I headed out the door. The Ray-Bans on top of my head held my chestnut-with-caramel-highlights shoulder length hair out of my face to reveal my workout-pink cheeks, and eyebrows with their perfect forty-dollars-a-month maintenance arch. Understated makeup and an age appropriate outfit, both would get the nod from one of those cable TV how-to-dress-yourself shows.

I pulled up to the local health food store. Taped to one of the double-glass doors, at eye level, hung an eight-by-ten-inch sheet of light green paper: The hand-lettered sign, with smiley faces for points at the bottom of the exclamation marks, read:

> Senior Day!
> If you are 55 or better!
> You deserve a discount!

I knew one of the young sales staff had written it. One of the same kids I always avoid in the store due to their ignorance of the merchandise. I have nothing against them and find it entertaining while they are trying to help. Ask for Ascorbic Acid and they'll direct you right to the Vitamin A.

After shopping for a few minutes, I gathered my supplements and got into the checkout line. While waiting, I scanned my items, added up the prices in my head, and estimated the total to be just under thirty dollars. Holding my purchases with one arm, I fished out a twenty and a ten from my wallet. I stood there trying not to stare at the tattoo of two skeletons having sex on the cashier's forearm. She was anorexic thin (Why do they hire unhealthy looking people to work in a store that's whole premise is to promote health?), and her boney chest screamed from under a ribbed, black tank top with the printed saying:

Just Because I Don't Care
Doesn't Mean I Don't Understand

Without speaking or even looking at me, she quickly added everything and placed the items and receipt in to a brown paper lunch bag. Still without moving her eyes, she said, "Eighteen sixty-five."

I have never been a math wizard, but this was way off. I thought, *OK, great, maybe the supplements are on sale.* I stuffed the ten-dollar bill in my pocket with the dollar thirty-five in change and headed toward the door.

My fingers touched its metal handle and my eyes caught the back of the green sign. My latent dyslexia kicked in, and those printed words slammed into my brain like a sledgehammer: Senior Discount! That skinny little twit had given me the senior discount without asking. And I'm not "55 or better"!

The mixture of embarrassment/anger/confusion made my neck and face burn. I kept my head down and pushed open the door, took a deep breath, walked straight toward the car, focused on my "Fresh Cherry" toenail polish shining up at me. I thought, *maybe she didn't apply the discount, or I must have missed some sale prices, or added it up wrong.*

I climbed into the car and slowly reached into the bag for the receipt. It uncoiled long and slow like a snake charmer's serpent. The bright blue soy ink reflected on the gray-whitish recycled paper. Printed under every dollar amount: SN DISC % -

I was stunned. I nearly tore the rearview mirror from its stem as I grabbed it to scan my face in a stack of cock-eyed rectangle increments. Forehead, eyes, nose, and lips...nothing I could see said "senior." I wondered what she saw.

I grappled with what to do. Go back in and demand to pay full price and produce my driver's license as proof? Would I make a fool of myself standing there in front of Ms. Bony Tattoo screaming that she had assumed incorrectly. Do I confront the manager and use my two-year age difference to give the store an additional eight dollars?

My mind kept repeating to me: *My mother gets discounts...I don't get discounts! I am too young for discounts! I am going to march back in there and demand to give them more money.*

Then I remembered my brother. A few days after his forty-eighth birthday, a waitress gave him an over-sixty discount. Years of hard work and hard living have left my brother looking sixty since he was forty. He was paying his check after breakfast with a bunch of much younger co-workers. The waitress was proud to announce he was entitled to pay a lower price and she made sure he got it. My brother, in a hushed tone, corrected her and said he was only forty-eight.

She apparently, with a loud laugh, said, "Come on, who are you trying to kid?"

My brother spoke again and a verbal battle ensued. Within moments his compatriots were laughing and choking on their cold coffee. My brother was so indignant and insulted. However, later he admitted he looked the part and didn't want to face it yet.

Sitting in the car, with a calm breeze cooling my anger, my sensible side kicked in and relaxation took over. What the heck, why be so upset? Eight bucks is eight bucks.

My eyes stared back at me in the mirror's reflection. I look pretty darn good for a senior. I won't be asking for discounts. However, if they are freely given, I won't fight it either.

About the author:

LeeAnn Dickson lives and works in Northern California. She is married to a wonderful and patient man and their family includes two Golden Retrievers and two neurotic cats.

In addition to her real job, she is a freelance writer working for a Sierra Foothill's regional magazine.

She is a lifelong story teller and loves to write about past adventures. "Senior Discount" is a true story.

TRUTH AND CONSEQUENCES
©2009 by Kaye Sebastian

The sunset glinted through the sheer curtain, a light breeze tickling its hem so that it danced like a flirtatious girl. Bob's father stirred. A dry cough escaped through his parted lips. Bob saw his chance.

"Pop, are you awake?"

The old man squinted. "The light," he said. "Hurts."

Bob leaned over to the nightstand and switched off the lamp. "Better?"

The watery blue eyes opened. "Yeah."

Bob's father was slipping. Since the fall that shattered his hip, each day carried him closer to the end. Bob knew it. So did his father. They'd wasted years moment by moment. Bob couldn't wait any longer.

He edged closer to the frail figure on the bed, taking in the odors of sour breath and unwashed flesh. "Tell me the truth."

The old man shifted; the metal bed frame creaked. "What are you talking about?"

"You know," Bob insisted.

A gust of wind shot through the window, knocking a vase of flowers off the sill. Glass shattered across the linoleum floor. Neither man reacted.

Bob understood—he had to play bad cop, as he had innumerable times with other suspects. "Sylvia Masterson," he said. "November 5, 1964. Stabbed in her living room." He paused.

"Unsolved."

There was, finally, a hint of recognition in his father's eyes. Fleeting, but there. Bob felt the familiar thrill of cornering a suspect. He went on. "No fingerprints, Pop. Just one hair."

The old man raised a bony, blue-veined hand to the top of his bald head. It reminded Bob of old photos of his father hamming it up at the club, one hand perched on his head, another on his hip in a foppish pose. Now it was pathetic.

Bob's father dropped his hand to the frayed white blanket. "What do you want to know?" he asked.

"Everything."

"I met Sylvia at a party in the fall of '60. She had great gams. I loved her." Another cough wracked the old man's body.

"You OK?" Bob offered his father water in an ochre-colored institution-issued cup.

Bob's father pushed the cup away. He caught his breath. "I saw her on weekends, after work, whenever I could."

Bob said nothing.

"She was worth the risk."

"So what happened?"

"Damn bed sores," he said, struggling to push himself up on his pillow, like an actor taking center stage before his monologue. "Move this friggin' thing," he croaked in exasperation, pulling a second pillow from beneath him. Bob threw the pillow to the end of the bed.

"Pop," Bob said, in a tone that lacked love or respect. "Quit stalling."

Bob's father pursed his lips, cleared his throat, and feebly snapped his fingers. Superstition taking over, Bob thought. It's the trifecta—lips, throat, hands—just like he's back at the casino, getting ready to roll the dice.

"She wanted to leave me."

Could it be that simple? Death over a break-up?

"And?"

A malevolent smile spread slowly across the face. Bob's father clammed up.

Screw him, Bob thought. He didn't care that Sylvia had left behind a daughter, Jeannie, who had come to Bob at the station a year before, begging for the case to be reopened.

"There's DNA now," Jeannie said. "Surely something can be done." She was a petite blonde, still youthful and achingly vulnerable at forty-nine. Yet she was persistent, visiting him every Tuesday like clockwork, always with her polite but firm request and theories of what might have happened to her mother. Six months after the visits, Jeannie caught him in a moment of weakness. He invited her to lunch, and she opened up to him about the stigma of being a murder victim's daughter, trying to escape the case by leaving town at seventeen, only to be pulled back by the unresolved conflict in her life. Bob listened, quietly comforted Jeannie, and then slept with her.

The next day, he reopened the most infamous cold case in Westville, Pennsylvania's history. He lugged the evidence boxes from the police station basement and spread their contents out on a rickety conference room table. The crime-scene photos showed 35-year-old Sylvia knifed almost to the point of being unrecognizable, splayed out on her living room floor, her clothes in tatters. It was a brutal crime in which the passion of the murderer was spelled out in the cuts to Sylvia's face and upper body, and in the shredding of her dark dress.

The photos and interview reports took Bob back to the scene in the kitchen when, at twelve, he read an article in the local paper about the case. He asked his mother what happened. "Sylvia Masterson was a whore," his mother said. "She deserved what she got."

Bob had no direct memory of the case. He was two years old in 1964; Jeannie was five when the crime occurred, but she was with her grandmother the evening of the murder.

According to the case files, there was no sign of forced entry. Bob guessed that Sylvia knew her killer. It was instinct, but fate helped out. The week after lunch with Jeannie, Bob's mother died of an aneurysm. A month later, he moved Pop to the nursing home and started the slow process of sifting through his parents' belongings.

In the back of their bedroom closet, he found the box. It looked like the other shoe boxes Bob had unearthed among his mother's possessions. He expected to find yet another outdated pair of high heels, barely worn, for the Salvation Army pile. Instead, the box held yellowing newspaper clippings about the Masterson case. The clippings weren't unusual, but the photos were. Crisp black and white shots of Sylvia Masterson laughing, her pouty lips teasing the rim of a wine glass; swooning in front of a microphone; posing coyly with laughing dark eyes, and in a low-cut dress. Amid the photos, he also found a swatch of navy-blue jersey fabric. He took the box and its contents to the station, locked them away, and did the only thing that made sense: took a gamble.

"Do you recognize this?" he asked Jeannie, holding out the swatch.

Jeannie lifted the navy-blue fabric from his hand. "Where did you get this?"

"Is it your mother's?"

Jeannie brought the fabric to her face. She breathed in deeply, lingering over the fabric before answering.

"I can smell her perfume." She looked at Bob; he could see hope spark in her eyes. "What does it mean?" she asked.

"Possibly new evidence."

The case progressed quickly. Bob deduced that he had a suspect. The fabric swatch in his father's possession put him at the scene of the crime. Bob toyed with having DNA tests run on the hair found at the scene, but held off. He didn't want to finger his father; he wanted a confession.

"Visiting hours end in ten minutes, Mr. Cleveland."

Bob turned and nodded at the perky nurse. He moved back to his father. Enough is enough, he thought. The old man would never see jail time now anyway. Bob had nothing to lose, and he had sworn to Jeannie that he'd catch her mother's murderer.

Bob grasped his father's shoulders. "Since you won't talk, Pop, let me tell you how I think it went down." He leaned over the old man, staring into the blue eyes that were so like his own. "You killed Sylvia because she threatened to leave you. You couldn't take the humiliation of rejection. She was beautiful, desirable, and you were nothing to her..."

Bob's father spat at him. "You don't know shit, Bobby."

"I know, Pop. You're a liar, a gambler, a cheat..."

"I ain't a murderer."

Emotion overtook Bob as years of contempt for his father bubbled over. In the hospital bed, now nearly helpless, lay the man who had defined Bob's early life, a man he'd battled with in adolescence and from whom he'd finally broken away by choosing a life in law enforcement, miles away from his father's philandering and petty crimes. "You cheated on Mom."

"She wasn't your mother!"

Bob released his father's shoulders. "What the hell are you talking about?"

His dad gasped for breath. "Your mother, the woman you think was your mother. She wasn't." The breaths came in short bursts. "I went to Sylvia's house that night. She was wearing the blue dress I bought her. I begged her not to dump me, but she said she'd had enough. Enough running around, hiding, lying about you."

"Me?"

"My wife couldn't have children," his father spoke, slipping back in time. "She never asked how I got you. I had her sign some fake form I typed up, and that was it. You were our baby. You were hers." His father's eyes closed. "But you weren't. You were Sylvia's."

Bob saw himself as a speck of dust floating in the last light filtering through the curtain. The curtain beckoned. He wanted to jump through it to the street below. But the old man in the bed kept talking.

"Sylvia wanted you back. She told me I'd stolen you, threatened to go to the cops, to take you from us. Your mother was listening at the open window. She charged in with the knife. Then we got the hell out of there, left Sylvia on the floor..."

"Where was I?" Bob asked.

"In the car," his father answered. Then, with the faintest hint of a plea, "She did it because of you. My cheating didn't matter, but when she heard Sylvia's plan to get you back, she snapped. Bobby, you were everything to her."

Bob paced. The industrial gray walls closed in on him. His thoughts narrowed. Sylvia was his birth mother, murdered by the woman he thought was his mother. He was a lie. He was a bastard. He was.... Jeannie!

"God."

"What?" his father asked.

Bob buried his face in his hands. "Jeannie Masterson, she came to the station, asked me to re-open the case."

His father's mind, still sharp, guessed the rest. "Christ almighty," he said with renewed gusto. "You're messing around with Sylvia's daughter? You're screwing your sister!" The laughter started low in the old man's belly, then swam out of him in waves, filling the room.

Bob couldn't breathe. He grabbed the pillow from the foot of the bed. "Pop," he said, "Shut up!"

"Oh, this is rich," the old man said, gasping.

Bob pushed the pillow into his father's face, bearing down with the full weight of his 220-pound frame. With each writhing squirm of the body under the pillow, Bob released forty-six years of pain: His parents' marriage teetering on financial ruin brought on by gambling; the whispers of neighbors who witnessed his father's drunken tirades and frequent arrests; the taunts of other kids who sensed his vulnerability; the crushing inadequacy he still carried with him, always anticipating a jibe from his father.

"Visiting hours have ended. Please exit the building."

The voice on the loudspeaker broke Bob's concentration. He lifted the pillow. The old man's face wasn't contorted with pain or horror; a mild look of surprise played across the features.

Disappointment funneled through Bob. In the end, he wanted Pop to suffer. Still, this time, Bob had the last word.

About the author:

Kaye Sebastian is a Philadelphia, PA-based writer whose passion is thriller fiction. She credits Scribes Valley with sparking her interest in "short stories with a twist," which developed through her submissions to the U-Write-It Online Challenge. Kaye's flash fiction story "The Collectible" received an honorable mention in the *Writers Weekly* 24-hour short story competition in July 2008 and her story "Six Minutes" is featured in the summer 2008 issue of *Mysterical-E* mystery e-zine. Her Scribes Valley entry, "Truth and Consequences," has its roots in real-life. Kaye belongs to the Chestnut Hill Writer's Group. At present, she is venturing into a new genre as she works on a screenplay based on one of her flash fiction stories.

THE RESTORER
©2009 by Bill Westhead

Despite having spent four years at art school, Jonathan Watson-Smythe had never had the courage to try to earn his living by being a painter. Although he continued to long for a life of leisure on some tropical island, painting for his own amusement, he had, instead, opted for the steadier, but less romantic occupation of restoration. Over a period of time he had established a reputation as a meticulous restorer of fine art.

He was a small man of indeterminate age, anywhere between thirty and fifty with long, graying fair hair that continually fell down over his penetrating blue eyes.

"It's magnificent," he said, standing on tiptoe and gazing in awe at the landscape hanging above the fireplace in the Great Hall of Runscord Manor. Then, realizing his words were totally inadequate to describe this masterpiece, added, "But what else would you expect from a master like Cezanne?"

Lord Runscord, who stood a full foot taller than Jonathan, nodded his gray head in agreement. "As you so rightly say, Mr. Watson-Smythe, what else would you expect?"

"Has it been in your family long, sir?" Jonathan asked.

"According to the provenance, my grandfather bought it from an estate sale in France in 1920 and it has been in the family ever since."

"Ah, you have the provenance, then," Jonathan said. "That makes it even more valuable. As you know, I am not an expert, but as an original I guess it would at least bring between three and four million pounds if it were to come up for auction. But then, sir, you did not ask me here for an evaluation, so in what way may I be of service to you?"

"This picture has been hanging here since it first came into the family and, as you can see, it has collected the dust of ages, plus the smoke and grit from many a fire. It needs restoring to its original state, and I understand from Sir Reginald White at the Tate you are one of the top art restorers in the country."

Jonathan bowed slightly and smiled at the compliment.

"I would like you to give me an estimate for the work," Lord Runscord continued.

"May we take it down so I can study it in more detail?" Jonathan asked.

Carefully the two men unhooked the three-foot by two-foot oil on canvas painting and lowered it onto the large oak table.

"It's certainly covered in grime," Jonathan said as his long sensitive fingers caressed the surface before lifting the top end to examine the back of the canvas. It was a full ten minutes before he looked up.

"Well?" Runscord said.

"Of course, it can be restored, but it will take some considerable time and I estimate the cost would be in the region of thirty to fifty thousand pounds."

Lord Runscord looked at Jonathan and rubbed his chin. "Um," he said in a non-committal way. "With the way the so-called aristocracy are taxed these days and the number of paintings I have that need restoration, I'm not sure I can afford to spend that much on one."

"While I would be pleased to do the work and come to some agreement regarding payment, maybe you would like a second opinion," Jonathan suggested, not trying to hide the disappointment in his voice.

Runscord looked at the little man and smiled. "No," he said finally. "You have been recommended and it's you I want to do the work. We can discuss the terms later."

"Thank you, sir, for your confidence, and I will make arrangements in the next few days to have the picture taken round to my studio."

Watson-Smythe picked up his coat and hat from the hallstand. "Perhaps," he said as he opened the front door, "when they pick up the picture, you would be good enough to make sure the provenance is attached so everything is kept together?"

Three weeks later Jonathan started the restoration, and six weeks after that found him seated at an easel, facing a blank canvas. The Cezanne landscape, now restored to its original condition, was displayed on a second easel to his right. Despite his reluctance to paint for a living, Watson-Smythe was an excellent painter in his own right and here was his opportunity to make the fortune for which he yearned.

It took him two weeks of painstaking effort to produce a copy of the landscape that even, in his opinion, an expert would have difficulty in detecting as a forgery. In another week, he had forged a copy of the provenance. He smiled as he carried the original landscape, with the provenance taped to the back, up to the attic and leaned it carefully against an inside wall. Later that same day Jonathan called Lord Runscord to say the restored painting was ready for delivery.

"Excellent, excellent," Lord Runscord, said rubbing his hands together as he stood back and viewed the vivid colors and exciting patterns of the restored picture, which was once again hanging over the fireplace. Then he stepped up onto the hearth and examined the painting more closely with the aid of a magnifying glass. "I see you have repaired the minute hole in the top right-hand corner so expertly I can't even find it," Runscord said as he stepped down and clapped Jonathan on the back. "You, sir, have done a wonderful job."

"I'm glad you're pleased with the work," Jonathan said, handing him the fake provenance. "Now, as regards the account."

Taking Jonathan by the arm, the two men retired to Lord

Runscord's study. It was a typical man's room from the Victorian era. An age-old odor of pipe and cigar tobacco pervaded the air and large bookcases holding dust covered leather bound volumes covered the oak-paneled walls.

Without saying a word Runscord strode over to a cabinet and poured a couple of shots of whiskey into two exquisite glass tumblers. He offered one to Jonathan before seating himself in a large comfortable armchair and indicating Jonathan take the other. After half an hour in these amicable surroundings, they finally agreed on a price of forty thousand pounds to be paid over a period of four months.

Watson-Smythe left the house, the first check for ten thousand pounds tucked safely in his breast pocket. A worried frown creased his forehead as he climbed into his car. *Strange,* he thought, *despite the close scrutiny I gave his original painting I never saw a hole, no matter how small. I must be slipping.* His one hope was that Lord Runscord would not take the picture down to examine the non-existent repair. Still, there was no time to lose.

Back at the studio, Jonathan rushed up to the attic and began to crate the original Cezanne, making sure the provenance was still taped to the back. By the next day the crate was on its way to Angelo Galliano in Milan. Although Jonathan had never met the man, he knew Angelo by reputation as being one of the top European art dealers and held in high esteem by the major art galleries of the world. He also knew that some private collectors were constantly in contact with the Italian, only too eager to purchase original works of art with little regard as to how they had come onto the market.

Three weeks later, following a phone call from Angelo, an excited Watson-Smythe was on a flight from London to Milan. *If I can persuade Angelo to pay me half the value of the painting and deposit that in a bank in the Cayman Islands, I am set up for life,* he thought as the plane lifted off. He spent the rest of the flight calculating how to invest his fortune. The Caribbean was becoming more and more attractive by the minute.

Angelo, a large rotund man in his early sixties, was waiting for him in the airport lounge. "Welcome to Milan," he said, extending his hand to Jonathan. Along with his many other attributes, Angelo spoke excellent English. "I am most pleased to meet you Mr. Watson-Smythe, although, of course, your reputation precedes you."

What a pompous man, Jonathan thought, *but I can put up with that if he pays the price.*

Angelo linked his arm through that of Jonathan's and hustled him through the airport. Outside, he hailed a taxi and gave the driver the address of his gallery.

"Your Cezanne is displayed in my private gallery upstairs," Angelo said as he led his guest through glass doors and along a wide corridor.

At each step, Jonathan's mouth became drier and drier and his heart beat faster and faster. He could hardly contain his excitement. Although the private gallery was a small room, Jonathan gasped when he saw it. Each wall was covered with neatly displayed masterpieces by Monet, Manet, Renoir, and many other renowned painters of years gone by. The Cezanne hung on the far wall.

"I thought you would be interested," Angelo said, a semblance of a smile flitting across his flabby face. "I gather you wish me to sell your painting?"

At a loss for words, Jonathan nodded. All he could think about was the sandy beaches and azure blue seas of the Caribbean.

"It may take me a little time to find a buyer," Angelo continued. "I am sure you realize these transactions cannot be rushed. But I will see what I can do."

"Wouldn't one of the major art galleries be interested in an original Cezanne?" Jonathan said.

"Of course," Angelo agreed, as he made towards the gallery door, "if it was an original."

"But it is!" Jonathan shouted. Suddenly the gallery started to spin and he had to put his hand on the doorframe to steady himself. "The provenance I sent with it proves it so, does it not?"

"Come with me, I have something to show you," Angelo said as he led the way down the stairs.

The two men entered a brightly lit room, tastefully decorated and fitted with modern furnishings. Angelo seated himself behind a large glass-topped desk and, with a nonchalant wave of his hand, suggested his visitor take the chair alongside him. In silence, the art dealer rummaged through a drawer and finally produced a large color photograph.

"That's my original painting," Jonathan said as Angelo pushed the photograph in front of him.

"Maybe yes and maybe no," Angelo said. "Let's take this back to the gallery and compare the two."

Jonathan's heart sank and his mind was in a whirl as they retraced their steps. With photograph in hand, he started to compare it to the painting, meticulously tracing every detail of color and line.

"I have some business I must attend to," Angelo said after a few minutes. "Clearly you will want to take your time. Please come back to my office when you have finished."

With that he left the gallery.

I wonder if that minute hole Runscord mentioned is the key to this puzzle? Jonathan thought, searching the top right-hand corner. He found nothing there.

Two hours later, Jonathan made his way back to the office. He was still uncertain why Angelo was so sure the picture was a forgery. After painstakingly comparing the painting and photograph, he had found no discrepancies.

"Well," said Angelo as Jonathan entered.

"Although I am at a loss as to your reasoning, you have made it clear that you think the painting I sent you is a forgery," Jonathan said. He tried to keep his voice calm, despite his rising temper.

Angelo leaned his large frame back in the chair and tapped his fingertips together. The same semblance of a smile that Jonathan had noticed on their first visit upstairs flickered across the art dealer's face. "I am sorry to tell you, my friend, it is a forgery, as is the provenance."

Jonathan went white. Suddenly, the Caribbean dissolved into the streets of London and he felt himself sliding into a dark hole. He knew that as a forgery, the Cezanne was of no interest to the major art galleries and thought it probably only worth a few thousand pounds even if an unsuspecting private collector could be found.

"Why are you telling me it's a forgery? What proof do you have?" he said, his voice rising with each word. "I am sure you are wrong."

"No, my friend. I am not wrong," Angelo said quietly. "In my business we are always on the lookout for this sort of thing. The photograph I gave you is of your painting that, at this very moment, is hanging in my private collection of forgeries.

"You are telling me that all those paintings up there," Jonathan gasped, pointing in the direction of Angelo's private gallery, "are forgeries?"

"Yes, my friend, every single one, but I prefer to call them copies and excellent copies at that." There was a twinkle in Angelo's eyes and that enigmatic smile was back on his face. "But let us get back to your Cezanne. In 1919, six paintings thought to be the work of Cezanne were discovered in the attic of an old house in Aix which, of course, is where the painter lived during the latter part of his life."

Jonathan wiped a bead of sweat from his brow. Suddenly, he realized that the information Angelo was giving him coincided too neatly for his liking with the time and place of the Runscord purchase.

"The art world was all abuzz at this find. For three years the experts closely examined, discussed, and argued about the paintings. But, as you are no doubt aware," Angelo continued, "Cezanne had a unique light, feathery touch so, today, many of his oils feel almost like watercolors and, while some have come close, no one has yet been able to replicate this technique. Because of this, it was determined that all six paintings were, regrettably, forgeries. Surprisingly enough," Angelo pointed at the photograph, "we are not even sure that Cezanne ever painted this particular scene. If he did, then my guess is the original was probably stolen and hidden by the Nazis during the war."

The art dealer leaned over, opened an ornate box, and offered Jonathan a cigar before lighting one himself and inhaling deeply. "In 1972," he continued, "the present Lord Runscord's father offered this particular Cezanne to the Louvre. Knowing the history, the French were suspicious and, much to Runscord's surprise, turned down the offer."

"But what about the provenance?" Jonathan said, leaning forward with hands clenched.

"Even provenances have been known to be forged."

Jonathan knew, from his own experience, that Angelo was right. "All that time and effort and for what?" he muttered. "I'm going to make more out of restoring the damn thing than in selling it."

"Do not give up my friend," Angelo said, a touch of sympathy in his voice. "It's an excellent painting and I am sure I can sell it to one of the less scrupulous private collectors I know in New York. Price?" He shrugged his shoulders, "If I ask too much he won't buy it and if I ask too little he'll smell a rat, as they say. Perhaps somewhere in the range of half to three quarters of a million, who knows?"

Jonathan' face brightened. It was far more than he had hoped for. He was about to leave when he decided to ask what had aroused Angelo's suspicions in the first place.

"Ah," Angelo said rubbing his hands together. "As soon as I saw the provenance stating that Lord Runscord's grandfather had bought it at an estate sale in France in 1920, I began to have doubts. That old rogue was a well-known collector of fakes and then, if necessary, finding someone to forge suitable provenances. I have been to Runscord Manor on a few occasions and photographed a number of paintings there. Despite all the provenances I have been shown on these visits, I doubt if there is an original painting in the house. I don't know if the present Lord Runscord is aware of this, but it would not surprise me if he wasn't just like his grandfather."

So, Jonathan thought, *Runscord has just swapped out one fake for another. How very appropriate.*

"By the way," Angelo continued, staring straight at Jonathan, "how did you come to be in possession of this painting? According to the provenance, fake or otherwise, it still belongs to Lord Runscord."

The question caught Jonathan by surprise, although he realized, too late, that he should have been prepared for it. Now he was trapped. There was no way out but the truth. He gulped twice before starting to tell the whole sordid story.

"You know," Angelo said kindly when Jonathan had finished, "you must be an excellent painter yourself if Lord Runscord could not differentiate between his original fake and your copy. Despite his doubtful dealings he is quite a connoisseur. By the way, did he say how well you had repaired a small hole in the painting?"

Jonathan was dumbfounded. "Yes," he said after a long pause. "How on earth did you know that?"

"He's inherited that old trick from his grandfather," Angelo said, a broad grin lighting up his flaccid face. "The old man used to make the same remark and watch for a reaction from the restorer. If he looked the slightest bit concerned, the old Lord immediately became suspicious and questioned him more closely until certain the restored painting was the original. Clearly you passed the test and Lord Runscord, apparently, has no idea that you swapped out his painting for a copy which, of course, you have just admitted doing. But then all's fair in love and war and, believe me, the art world can be a war zone at times."

Jonathan smiled. It felt good to have come clean and Angelo did not seem annoyed or even amazed by his story.

"Well," Jonathan said, rising to his feet, "I have taken up enough of your time and I thank you for your courtesy."

"It's been pleasure meeting you, Mr. Watson-Smythe." Angelo extended his hand. "I will be in touch when I have a buyer."

"After all I've told you, you still intend to try and sell the picture?" Jonathan said as he shook the proffered hand.

"Of course. It would be a shame to discard such an excellent copy. After all, it does have some history attached to it. As I said earlier, you are an excellent painter in your own right. Why don't you send me some of your own work? There's no reason for you to spend your time copying others."

"You deal with forgeries?" Jonathan said in amazement.

Angelo smiled. "Not forgeries," he said. "As I said earlier, I prefer to call them excellent copies and I price them accordingly. The world is full of such copies and they give pleasure to many. So, I hope we can do business again someday."

"Am I a forger?" Jonathan wondered as the Boeing 727 winged its way over France. *"Or did I just make a copy of a copy?"*

He still had no answer to his question as they touched down at London's Heathrow airport.

Perhaps with Angelo Galliano's help, I could supplement my income by selling my own work as well as copies of masterpieces, he thought as he pushed open the door to his studio.

The dream of living in the Caribbean was still alive.

About the author:

This is Bill Westhead's *fourth* time as a finalist in the Scribes Valley Short Fiction Contest. His previous stories, "Romeo and Sierra's Last Mission," "Cruel Justice," and "Adventure in the Caucases" were finalists in 2005, 2006, and 2007 and published in the anthologies of those years: *They Do Exist!, Mind Trips Unlimited,* and *Destination Elsewhere.*

Born in England, Bill and his family emigrated to Waycross, Georgia in 1973. With their children having fled the nest to start their own families, he and his wife continue to live in Waycross with their dog Ben and cat Oscar.

A member of Southeastern Writers Association and Coastal

Writers Group, he has published four historical novels *Once in Old Frederica Town, Confederate Gold, Clogs,* and its sequel *The Mill.* His work has also been published in *Cricket, Animal Tales, Chicken Soup* series, the *O, Georgia!* Anthology, *Crafts n Things* and several trade magazines. Apart from novels and short stories, he also writes a monthly theatre column, "Footlights", for area and local newspapers.

He has completed his fifth book *Not My War*, a memoir of his time as a child in England during World War II and is currently in discussion about the book with a publisher.

When not writing, he divides his time between his Bonsai collection and the Waycross Area Community Theatre.

FORTY
©2009 by Dan Sullivan

By the time Tanya Culpepper turned fifteen, she had become what her grandmother called "top-heavy." On her knees each night, Tanya never failed to praise God for His blessings and to thank Him for them. In spite of her ample endowments, however, Tanya never strayed—not even one little bit—from the most scrupulous modesty in behavior or attire. There was, however, only so much that modesty could suppress. So it was not at all unusual, whenever Tanya entered a room full of people, for the men to stop talking and start looking and, by degrees, migrate over to where Tanya stood; usually alone, since women didn't care all that much for her. So, with this in mind, Myrtle McCarty called her godchild and best friend's daughter who had just turned twenty-four.

"Tanya, hon, I need a huge favor from you."

"What's that, Aunt Myrtle?"

"Next Sunday is Gordy Armbruster's fortieth, and I've kind of pulled together a little surprise party for him. He's my godson, and I feel I owe that to him. You got my invitation, right?

"I'm not going."

Myrtle resisted the urge to fuss or quarrel, but she wasn't surprised. Tanya declined almost every invitation and left the house, as a rule, only for work, Sunday services, Bible study on Wednesday evenings, choir practice on Thursdays, and food shopping for her grandmother the first thing on Saturday mornings, long before the nine o'clock bunch starts rolling in.

Myrtle ignored what Tanya said and continued. "Like I said, Gordy's turning forty so I wanted to go all out. I got a hall rented, bought sodas and beer, Bunch Allbritton's going to fry chicken and bring pasta—his favorite. Martha, Gordy's stepsister, has pledged to bring stuffed ham and some of those deviled eggs of hers. I figure the three of us have already laid out close to three hundred dollars. That doesn't even include the cost for the three bushels of soft-shell crabs the Trossbachs down at Point Lookout have promised me. I got everything all lined up for that fool's surprise birthday party—even dreamed up a nice little lie to get him there. Now everything's a great big mess. First he accepts and then he goes and tells me he can't come. Says he's got work next Sunday and can't get out of it. Now just what in God's name does *an insurance agent* have to do on a Sunday that he can't get out of?"

"Why not just tell Gordy you're having a party for him and he's got to come?"

Myrtle moved the receiver about a foot from her ear and moved her head slowly from side to side as if she were appealing to an imaginary, equally exasperated audience.

"It's a surprise party, Tanya. A *surprise*. *That's* why I can't tell him."

Myrtle never accused Tanya of being in the Gifted and Talented Program, although in reality she had been a straight-A student, yet Myrtle also realized that her own voice was getting a bit too edgy to be asking for a favor, so she decided to tone it down a bit.

"Tanya, this whole thing has me on edge, hon. See, I need you to do me a favor and invite Gordy out on Sunday and get him to the surprise party."

"But he's got to work."

Again, Myrtle moved the receiver away from her ear and rolled her eyes for the benefit of her imaginary, long-suffering sympathizers. "That's where you come in, Tanya. That's going to kinda be your role: to invite him. He'll go if you ask him. I figured with your...." Myrtle cut her sentence short and started rummaging through her word drawer for a discreet way of explaining Tanya's effectiveness with men.

"Influence?"

"That's exactly what I mean, hon, the *influence* that you have over...." Myrtle left unsaid the rest of what Tanya knew and what Myrtle was thinking: *just about half of the entire population of Southern Maryland.*

"But I don't like Gordy. He drinks too much, and when he does he's flirty. He never goes to church, and frankly he needs to brush his teeth more often."

"Well, all that's true. Truer words were never spoken. Gordy's not going to star in a soap opera any time soon, but listen, you don't have to stay. Just get him there. Once he's there and surprised, you can do whatever you want: stay, go, leave early, stay late, leave early and come back. Whatever you want, hon. Just get him there. If you need to leave right away, I'll have somebody carry you home. Please do this for your Aunt Myrtle."

There was a lengthy pause at the other end, and Myrtle knew enough not to push it any harder at this point-just let the girl take her time.

"O.K., Aunt Myrtle, what's Gordy's number?"

Down to his boxer shorts and flip flops, a man with bushy orange hair and white skin not unlike the underbelly of a rockfish, lay on his bed and, with mischievous blue eyes, regarded the rotating blades of the overhead fan. Their slow methodical movement was nearly hypnotic and easily invited Gordon Sloan Armbruster to drift back and savor his most recent and, arguably, his best practical joke—ever. Two weeks earlier, he had helped Pee Wee Hudson, a diminutive, jittery chain-smoker in his fifties, who was working on his fourth divorce, move into a top floor unit of the Cedar Lane Apartments of Leonardtown.

With the last cardboard box stacked in Pee Wee's new living room, Gordy surveyed the apartment and asked offhandedly, "Does your rent include the cost of electric?"

"Yes."

"That's a relief."

"How so?"

"Well, you'll probably be keeping your lights on most of the time after you go to bed at night. And if you had to pay for it all yourself...."

"Why on earth would I keep my lights on at night?"

"Didn't they tell you at the rental office?" Gordy corrected himself. "What a dumb question! Of course, they wouldn't tell you."

"Tell me what?"

"About the last tenant."

"Don't you play with me, Gordy. What about the last tenant?"

With feigned reluctance, Gordy then proceeded to inform Pee Wee that the previous tenant, a recently divorced man in his fifties—not unlike Pee Wee—had been the victim of a grisly murder shortly after moving in. "Funny thing, Pee Wee. There was no forced entry, and all the doors and windows were locked, including the front door. *Locked from the inside,* mind you, with the chain lock still on! That's what has the Sherriff's Department stumped. How could that happen to a guy who lived alone unless the murderer was still there or could pass through walls?"

The color began to drain from Pee Wee's face, and his hangdog eyes had become more desperate with each detail.

Gordy forced a brave smile. "But I'm sure everything will be just fine, Pee Wee. It's probably just a silly-ass rumor. You know how those things start. Now you take care, but keep your lights on, just in case. They tell me spirits can't stand light."

Every night for the next week, after closing time at *Cadillac Jack's Night Club,* Gordy made it a point to pass Pee Wee's apartment building. Every night, he saw all the lights on in the unit and the silhouette of a small man pacing back and forth with a cigarette in his mouth and a baseball bat on his shoulder. And every night, Gordy had to pull off onto the shoulder until he could get his breathless laughter under control before getting back on

Route 5. The last Gordy heard, Pee Wee had asked one of his ex's to let him crash on a couch in her basement, "Just for a night or two."

The blades continued their hypnotic rotation. Gordy guffawed as he pictured Pee Wee's silhouette, but its memory now presented a problem as well a challenge, a challenge for him to reach even greater heights of tomfoolery.

Gordy needed something special, something really *remarkable* so that no one in the family would ever forget the day that Gordon Sloan Armbruster turned forty and was still standing strong as the biggest rascal in Southern Maryland. After reflecting about it for several more rotations of the fan, Gordy decided: yes, he *would* get one of the girls at "The Chopping Block" in Great Mills to give him a Mohawk haircut. He was considering whether to add a dashiki to the overall effect as he entered the Jolly Hunters' Hall at 3 p.m. the following Sunday. He couldn't wait to see the reaction the haircut and the African tunic would cause on the extended Allbritton-Armbruster family, most of whom sat to the far right of each and every aisle.

And about the surprise party itself, Gordy knew exactly what was up. Nobody had to call him out of the rain more than once. He knew when his Aunt Myrtle called just what they were planning and, of course, he would, in the end, show up. Still, that didn't mean he couldn't create a little devilment in the meantime. So, after initially agreeing to come next Sunday for his Aunt Myrtle's bogus "family business meeting," Gordy called back a little later to give his heartfelt regrets. Duty called, he told his Aunt Myrtle. A client would only conduct business on the golf course, and Gordy frankly needed the sale. Gordy wouldn't leave his Aunt Myrtle hanging too long, however. She was, after all, close to seventy and the McCartys weren't known for cardiovascular systems that were all that good.

Gordy was still on his back staring at the overhead fan when his cell phone started playing Chopin's "Funeral March."

"Gordy? This is Tanya Culpepper."

Gordy swallowed hard, sat up, and swung his legs over the side of the bed. He shifted the phone to the other ear. Not even in his wildest dreams.... "Tanya, what can I do for you, hon?"

Tanya then asked Gordy if he could do her a huge favor and escort her to her company's picnic the following Sunday. "We're supposed to bring somebody, but if you don't want to go...."

"Just hold on there, Tanya. It would be an honor to escort you next Sunday to your company picnic."

On her knees that night, Tanya begged the Lord's forgiveness for telling a bold-faced lie, and she pleaded with Him to *please, PLEASE* let her get as sick as a dog so she wouldn't have to wind up next Sunday with Gordy and his lame jokes and his bad breath. Amen.

SURPRISE!! SURPRISE!!

As Tanya and Gordy entered the Jolly Hunters' Club, the birthday boy raised his eyebrows and opened his mouth to communicate his *utter* astonishment, all to the delight and relief of his Aunt Myrtle and the other ladies in the family. Gordy, *sans* Mohawk and *sans* dashiki, was dressed conservatively—at least by Gordy Armbruster standards: flip-flops, Levis, and a red Hawaiian shirt with huge white and yellow flowers splashed throughout the design. To Gordy's way of thinking, a Mohawk and a dashiki couldn't begin to match being seen with Tanya Culpepper to memorialize the day he turned forty. As family and friends gathered around Gordy, Tanya took the opportunity to slip off to a corner. She was dressed for the occasion as she did for every rare social event she got dragged to: a brown, unrevealing pants suit and flats. Her dark hair was pulled back in a ponytail, revealing large gray eyes, a peaches-and-cream complexion, and fine features, making her face appear more like a teenager's than that of a woman in her mid-twenties. And, following the advice of her pastor's wife, she wore no makeup, which only made her look even fresher and more appealing.

Her attire did not go unnoticed by a less-than-generous second female cousin of Gordy's, who stage-whispered to no one in particular, "Tanya's like one of them Taliban women—doesn't show a whole lot. *Right, Tanya! Sure thing!* Who in the world does *she* think she's fooling?"

Card tables covered in white paper cloth ringed the hall. In the center, several long rectangular tables had been pushed together and displayed fried chicken—piles and piles of it, pots of spaghetti with thick marinara sauce just the way Gordy liked it, an orange hillock of steamed crabs, several bowls of potato salad, a platter of deviled eggs, and a serving dish of ham stuffed with kale.

Coolers of sodas and beer were at either end of the buffet tables, and in the far-right corner of the hall was a pile of packages wrapped in colored tissue paper and bound with matching ribbons. And strung across the back wall was a white plastic banner, about three-feet high, with the words in red, block letters, *LORDY LORDY GORDY'S FORTY.*

Bunch Allbritton, a large, dimpled woman in lavender gingham and an aunt of Gordy's on his father's side, used her third-grade teacher's playground voice to get everyone's attention. "All right, everybody, let's start at the buffet and take a place so we can have the blessing."

Most everyone in turn laid siege to the buffet table and quickly took a seat at one of the card tables. The guest of honor looked around the hall for Tanya who was pretending to be busy in a back corner with some of the other ladies filling plastic cups with mixed fruit. He was starting to fear that his face time with Tanya would not be what the family would always remember about the day he turned forty. So, then he would have Nothing. Absolutely Nothing. No Mohawk. No dashiki. No Tanya. Gordy resignedly joined his second cousin U-Dean, a heavy young man with bad teeth, who wore a stained red World Wrestling Federation hat and a tee shirt with the replica of the Confederate flag on both front and back. The motto under the Confederate flag announced curiously "Fighting Terrorism for the Last Two Hundred Years." U-Dean's ample stomach spilled over the top of his Levis like a half-filled sandbag. He, too, was searching the hall for Tanya. Spotting her in a back corner, he leaned toward Gordy and leered.

"What's Tanya like, Gordy? How far you gotten with her so far?"

Gordy smiled lamely and looked toward the back of the hall. Meanwhile, Pee Wee Hudson sat down at their table and persisted in getting Gordy's attention. Livid stains of sleeplessness cupped Pee Wee's dark eyes.

"I checked with the Sherriff's Office, Gordy. Never was any murder in my 'partment. It was one of those hair-brained practical jokes of yours, wasn't it?"

Gordy furrowed his brow and pursed his lips in surprised skepticism. He felt the gears of one wheel starting to turn. "That's not what I heard from one of the Deputy Sheriffs. Who'd you talk to, Pee Wee?"

"You got to first base with her yet, Gordy?"

Bunch Allbritton now used her Park-Hall-Elementary-School-auditorium voice to get everyone's attention. "You all! The Reverend Buddy will now offer a blessing over the food."

The Reverend Buddy, another member in the extended Allbritton-Armbruster clan, was an eight-year old evangelist-healer from Calvert County who had his own radio show once a month on WPAX, spreading the gospel in a high-pitched, nasal voice just before the six a.m. boating forecasts. Standing on a folding chair, he began a prayer that would last several minutes and outlast the patience of all. By the third "Father, we just thank you," people began to fidget.

"Father, we just..."

"The Deputy said you were just pulling one of those stupid-ass jokes of yours again, Gordy. And I fell for it."

"Shoot, Gordy, I bet you haven't even left home plate yet, have you? I hate to break it to you, Gordy, but she don't seem interested at all. Why's she back in the corner with Aunt Myrtle?"

No Mohawk. No dashiki. No Tanya. If there were a Muse for rascals and practical jokers, Gordy would have invoked her aid...urgently.

"...we just thank you for the..."

"My boss said I could probably end up on Judge Alex or Judge Judy or one of them other TV judges and sue your fool ass for pain and suffering. I haven't gotten a good night's...."

"Now, if *I* was up at bat with her...but maybe sitting in an insurance office all day don't give you the right kind of energy. You know what I mean, Gordy? See, that's where I'm lucky. When I do have a job, I work with my hands...."

"...we just thank you, too, for Gordy..."

"I got plenty of energy, Gordy. Shoot, not even on first base yet? Downright pitiful."

The Reverend Buddy's blessing proceeded then to mention each and every member of the extended Allbritton-Armbruster family by first and last name. The Reverend Buddy did not fail to include in his thanksgiving friends of the family such as Tanya and Pee Wee, and then on to all the public servants of St. Mary's County, Maryland, all the men and women in the Sherriff's Department, the people in the Great Mills Fire and Rescue Department, the teachers.... The shifting and fidgeting intensified. There was even a murmured complaint or two, which Bunch shushed.

The Muse at last had hovered; and then on the power of her sudden inspiration, Gordy let forth a groan that could be heard over the Reverend Buddy's attenuated blessing now focused on the maintenance personnel in the St. Mary's County Public School System. Gordy bent forward in his chair, and buried his face in his plate of spaghetti.

Several of the ladies screamed. The Reverend Buddy stopped the blessing. Folding chairs were pushed aside and the guests started making their way to the guest of honor.

U-Dean reached over and raised Gordy's limp arm. He let it go before it fell back on the table. "Damn, Pee Wee. I think he's passed!"

"He can't die! Not before I get that fool on Judge Alex and get my pain and suffering. "

Gordy's face was still buried in his plate of spaghetti when U-Dean got the urge to smack Gordy. It wasn't the first time he had felt that way, but now he wanted proof whether Gordy had really passed or whether this was just one of his idiotic jokes. U-Dean cuffed Gordy gently on the side of the head and then half-punched his shoulder. Gordy remained motionless.

"Damn. He's gone, Pee Wee."

While U-Dean looked for Tanya, Pee Wee approached and began jabbing Gordy's arm. "No, you don't, Gordy. Don't you dare. I'll kill you if you die on me, not before I get my day in court on T.V."

U-Dean raised Gordy's limp arm a final time and let it fall back on the table. "Deader than a doorknob."

The others reached Gordy's table and began to circle it, but not too close. Myrtle and Bunch shouted for someone to call 911. Simultaneously, fifty cell phones began calling the St. Mary's County 911 system, overloading it so that no one got through at first.

So far in his ministry, the Reverend Buddy had never seen a dead person; not up close at least. He slipped through the crowd behind Gordy and, after reaching and then pulling back his hands several times, he finally touched his distant cousin gently on his shoulders. He wasn't cold or stiff. He was as warm as a kitten. The boy preacher predictably began to offer a prayer for his still-warm second cousin, when without warning, Gordy lifted his face from the plate, tendrils of spaghetti hanging limply from nose and earlobes, a mass of marinara sauce on the top of his head, and, with an unfixed stare, he stood with his arms extended. Gordy then began to moan and move with heavy, rocking steps toward U-Dean, who gaped at his cousin and turned as white as a ghost.

Bunch Allbritton, again in her school-auditorium voice, announced as if over a loud speaker, "Praise God! Buddy's raised Gordy from the dead!"

"*OOOOOOOOH!*"

With the same unfixed stare and arms extended stiffly in front of him, Gordy continued moaning and taking heavy rocking steps toward Pee Wee and U-Dean. The crowd around the table scattered. U-Dean knocked Pee-Wee out of the way and made a sudden move toward the exit, unaware of the patch of marinara sauce and spilled beer immediately in front of him. U-Dean took one step, one sorry misstep, before becoming air-borne. His right leg kicked out in front of him first, then the left. One observer later swore that for a good second or two, "the boy" was actually suspended in air, parallel to the floor, before he dropped like a stone on the linoleum.

Bunch was still praising the Lord for Buddy's miracle, "Brought back from the grave, Halleluiah!"

For most of the others, however, panic had set in; a few shoves, but none to speak of, really, mostly bumping and sidestepping. Tanya, who had been transfixed by Gordy's revival, suddenly "fell out" and lay prone several yards from U-Dean, also face up and motionless on the floor. One of the 911 calls had finally gotten through and, not long afterwards, the Great Mills Volunteer Fire and Rescue Department arrived on-scene. The deployment consisted of the Schmidt twins, recent male graduates from St. Mary's Ryken High School in Leonardtown, and Salina Gomez, a nineteen-year-old technician at Great Mills Animal Hospital, whom the twins called "hot." The team was under the able command of Battalion Chief Sky Breton, a man in his early thirties, who looked like a cherub on performance-enhancing supplements, although he never in all his born days put anything stronger than an aspirin in his body which he called "a temple of God."

When not managing Domino's Pizza, Battalion Commander Breton pursued three passions in his life: choir at the Great Mills Church of Christ where he was the lead tenor, power-lifting, and the volunteer fire department. Consistent with his training, Sky did not rush blindly into action but did what was called for first: assessment.

He surveyed the hall while the civilians were clamoring for him to "do something, *do* something." After careful assessment of the scene, he made his decision and led his team over to attend to Tanya. When that decision was later second-guessed by several female members of the family, Myrtle put things into a healthy perspective. "For the love of God, suppose you're a man and you got U-Dean and you got Tanya both lying face up on the floor, just who in the name of the holy Lord are you gonna tend to first? Use your brain, girl."

When Tanya opened her eyes, she looked up into the cherubic face of Sky Breton, who had waived off everyone else and was personally tending to her. He had one of her hands in his, and for one disoriented moment, Tanya felt she had reached eternal reward and was looking into the face of what she would later describe as "a welcoming angel of God." By degrees, she came to her senses and realized where she was and where she had seen that face so many times before: at the Great Mills Church of Christ where she, too, was a choir member. Both Sky and Tanya were secretly crazy about each other but painfully bashful. Both tried to hide their feelings for the other, avoiding each other with downcast eyes, averted glances, and wide circumlocutions as they left the church. And both had also prayed each and every night since the first time they had seen each other that the good Lord would, in His kindness, find a way to bring them together.

In spite of her protests that she was just fine, and in violation of just about every protocol in emergency medicine, Sky himself carried Tanya in his arms to a gurney and wheeled her out to the ambulance parked outside. It was en route that Sky finally worked up the nerve to ask her if she would do him the honor to go out for coffee after next Wednesday's Bible study. Tanya blushed and said that would be nice. Employing skills cultivated at Dominos, Sky slid her into the back of the ambulance.

Back inside, the Schmidt twins had finally noticed U-Dean and were arguing about which one would take his pulse and which one would check his heart rate. When U-Dean started to come to,

Gordy surveyed it all and concluded that, yes, he had outdone himself this time—in spite of Tanya. There was no way anybody would ever forget his fortieth. He then called out to no one in particular yet to everyone within earshot, "U-Dean's O.K. It was just his head."

The reaction wasn't what he had expected. No one laughed. No one turned his way. No one paid him any mind.

Salina raised one disapproving eyebrow and was about to join the twins, when she turned to Gordy and said, "It's not my place, mister, but a lot of people got hurt by all this. It's not the least bit funny." Salina joined the Schmidt twins in tending to U-Dean, whom they would soon shuttle off to the emergency room for observation.

Gordy stood alone as he finished wiping his face. His first reaction was to take offense at what she had said. *Who did she think she was?* But the more he thought about it, the more he agreed that the girl was right: a whole lot of people *had* gotten hurt by his antics today: Tanya and U-Dean who had both fallen out; and God only knew where Pee Wee had run off to and what his condition was; and then there was Aunt Myrtle and all the rest of the family—spared the emergency room but not the sting of Gordy's ingratitude and insensitivity.

Everyone but Gordy lent a hand in cleaning up, and not a single soul approached him or even cut their eyes over his way as he stood in the center of the hall. As his family and friends left the Jolly Hunters', they all made darn sure that they took as many of the leftovers as they could carry and took back their presents for Gordy. And who could blame them for that?

Without looking in his eyes, Myrtle McCarty handed the crumpled *LORDY LORDY GORDY's FORTY* banner to her godson and said softly, "You need to grow up, son."

That night under the rotating fan, Gordy thought long and hard about what it all meant and where he was really headed in life.

Forty! On the prowl every night at Cadillac Jack's until

closing. Hangover remedies every morning. Chasing lonely divorcees, scaring sawed-off little Pee Wee half to death, fancying he even had a ghost of a chance with girls half his age. Where had it all gone? Where was he going? Where would he be in a year— or five? Damn, he couldn't trick himself any longer and no amount of tomfoolery could turn back time.

He had a lot more thinking to do that night, but he knew his next steps had something to do with lots of apologies and lots of amends.

Things in real life seldom, if ever, work out as nicely as they do in romantic comedies, with all the right people together, with all the bad guys in their place, with the Lord in His heaven and all's right with the world, but they did here. Myrtle, in time, had to admit in all truthfulness that it was pretty darn funny to think of Gordy stomping like a zombie toward U-Dean and Pee Wee, and she finally got over her hurt and anger at her godson when he sent her a heart-felt note of apology and a check for $300. She said she'd forgive but never forget.

Sky and Tanya have been out on three dates so far, and he's just about ready to pop the question—whether it would be all right for him to put his arm around her shoulder the next time they go to the movies.

U-Dean finally got some sense in his head, admitted that *some* Hispanic immigrants, at least one or two of them, weren't that bad, and he enrolled in the College of Southern Maryland. He says he finally wants to make something of himself, perhaps become an emergency medical technician, like "that Spanish girl" Salina, who's up for promotion in the Great Mills Volunteer Fire and Rescue Department.

Pee Wee broke his lease at the Cedar Lane Apartments and has moved back in permanently with number four. They plan to see a counselor next week. Pee Wee's also fooling with the idea of resuming his *tae kwon do* lessons with Master Kim—just to get in shape, although a boost in his self-confidence wouldn't hurt either.

The Schmidt twins can vouch for the saying that good things come to those who wait: Salina's twin cousins, Maria and Magdelena, just arrived from EI Salvador, and they're even "hotter" than she is.

Bunch and the Reverend Buddy will no longer go so far as to say the boy preacher brought Gordy back from the grave, but they will claim, without any equivocation, that the Reverend Buddy helped bring his wayward cousin back to his senses on the day that Gordon Sloan Armbruster turned forty.

About the author:

Dan Sullivan teaches English literature and composition at St. Mary's Ryken High School in Leonardtown, Maryland. Dan has had three short stories published to date; the last placed second in the 2006 Scribes Valley Fiction contest, but he is most proud of his family—his wife Jamie, his daughter Laura, his son Mark, his two granddaughters Kyleigh and Erika, and his step-daughter Ploy who lives in Bangkok.

www.ingramcontent.com/pod-product-compliance
Lightning Source LLC
Chambersburg PA
CBHW061209170626
46809CB00003B/1304